Edward Jenkins

Ginx's Baby

His Birth and Other Misfortunes

Edward Jenkins

Ginx's Baby
His Birth and Other Misfortunes

ISBN/EAN: 9783337266875

Printed in Europe, USA, Canada, Australia, Japan

Cover: Foto ©Andreas Hilbeck / pixelio.de

More available books at **www.hansebooks.com**

His Birth and other Misfortunes.

A SATIRE.

BOSTON:

JAMES R. OSGOOD & CO.,

(LATE TICKNOR & FIELDS, AND FIELDS, OSGOOD, & CO.)

PREFACE.

CRITIC. — *I never read a more improbable story in my life.*

AUTHOR. — *Notwithstanding, it may be true.*

NOTE TO THE SECOND EDITION.

THREE or four weeks after the publication of "Ginx's Baby," the author is called upon by the publishers to revise it for a second edition. In this notoriety of the fortunes of "Ginx's Baby," the most deep and real satisfaction comes from the general recognition of the sincere and earnest purpose of the history. This sufficiently neutralizes the misunderstandings or misjudgments of some two or three critics.

To those who have criticised the book in the modern fashion, the author has only most gently to deprecate that they should have felt themselves constrained to make objections when they obviously had none to make. To take an instance: One not unkindly critic declares that the author "OFTEN mistakes invective for satire," — a remark so paradoxical as to require solution. The author is conscious of having deliberately used both invective and satire; but the error of confounding them he returns to the critic. The same judge observes, "The only man described in the book who has any indefinite (*quære*, definite?) remedies to propose for the diseases of modern civilization is a generous-hearted fanatic, rather than a judicious statesman;" and he records his suspicion that Sir Charles Sterling's most impracticable suggestions are "especially dear to the author." Did it not occur to the critic that the author intended to represent in Charles Sterling a "generous-hearted fanatic," and that his intention is clearly written on every page of the baronet's exaggerated talk? A man made an enthusiast by too keen a sensitiveness to wrong and sorrow is not an unnatural or unadmirable character: nay, much wisdom may play brightly through the thunder-clouds of his passion.

Lastly, the author desires to set himself right with the reader on one point in which it seems he is likely to be misunderstood. The editor of "The Spectator," otherwise applauding, had referred to the passage on the "Timbuctoo question," pp. 115, 116, as "utterly and basely wrong."   In "The Spectator" of June 4 appeared the following letter from the author; commending which to his readers and critics, he confides to their consciences the second edition : —

TO THE EDITOR OF "THE SPECTATOR."

SIR, — In your kindly notice of my little book on Saturday last, you did me an unintentional though an almost deserved injustice.   Will you allow me to relieve myself from it without doffing my *incognito ?*   You have read a passage on "the Timbuctoo question" as an expression of that extreme and ignoble radicalism which would subordinate the honor of the nation to its wealth.   Perhaps my incautious anger has left the passage open to that interpretation ; but I wish to disclaim it.   I revolt from that doctrine as much as you ; and, if you knew my name, you would perhaps recognize one who has publicly and practically striven to refute it.

My mind, when I wrote the passage referred to, was indignantly alert to the contrast between the fury, vigor, and sacrifice so quick for such an enterprise as that, and the mournful debility of zeal in the redress of our own home sorrows. I may be "sometimes unjust:" God knows I wish I were all untrue.   Besides, you will allow me to think, as I do, that a little politic management and expenditure might have rescued the Abyssinian captives without an expedition costing ten million pounds. Otherwise, I agree with you that a people unchary of its honor at any sacrifice is fit only to be enslaved by some nobler race.

I am, sir, &c.,

THE AUTHOR OF "GINX'S BABY."

CONTENTS.

PART I.

WHAT GINX DID WITH HIM.

		PAGE.
I.	Ab Initio	13
II.	Home, Sweet Home	15
III.	Work and Ideas	19
IV.	Digressive, and may be skipped without mutilating the History	21
V.	Reasons and Resolves	24
VI.	The Antagonism of Law and Necessity	25
VII.	Malthus and Man	29
VIII.	The Baby's First Translation	33

PART II.

WHAT CHARITY AND THE CHURCHES DID WITH HIM.

I.	The Milk of Human Kindness, Mother's Milk, and the Milk of the Word	35
II.	The Protestant Detectoral Association	41
III.	The Sacrament of Baptism	43
IV.	Law on Behalf of Gospel	44
V.	Magistrate's Law	49
VI.	Popery and Protestantism in the Queen's Bench	52
VII.	A Protester, but not a Protestant	55
VIII.	"See how these Christians love One Another!"	56
IX.	Good Samaritans, and Good-Samaritan Twopences	62
X.	The Force; and a Specimen of its Weakness	64
XI.	The Unity of the Spirit and the Bond of Peace	66
XII.	No Funds, no Faith, no Works	76
XIII.	In Transitu	77

12 CONTENTS.

PART III.

WHAT THE PARISH DID WITH HIM.

PAGE.

I. Parochial Knots; to be untied without Prejudice . . 79
II. A Board of Guardians 80
III. " The World is my Parish " 84
IV. Without Prejudice to Any One but the Guardians . . 85
V. An Ungodly Jungle 88
VI. Parochial Benevolence; and Another Translation . . 92

PART IV.

WHAT THE CLUBS AND POLITICIANS DID WITH HIM.

I. Moved on 95
II. Club Ideas 96
III. A Thorough-paced Reformer, if not a Revolutionary . 101
IV. Very Broad Views 106
V. Party Tactics, and Political Obstructions to Social
   Reform 113
VI. Amateur Debating in a High Legislative Body . . . 119

PART V.

WHAT GINX'S BABY DID WITH HIMSELF.

The Last Chapter 123

GINX'S BABY.

PART I.

WHAT GINX DID WITH HIM.

I.—Ab Initio.

THE name of the father of Ginx's Baby was Ginx. By a not unexceptional coincidence, its mother was Mrs. Ginx. The gender of Ginx's Baby was masculine. On the day when our hero was born, Mr. and Mrs. Ginx were living at Number Five, Rosemary Street, in the city of Westminster. The being then and there brought into the world was not the only human entity to which the title of "Ginx's Baby" was or had been appropriate. Ginx had been married to Betsy Hicks at St. John's, Westminster, on the twenty-fifth day of October, 18—, as appears from the "marriage lines" retained by Betsy Ginx, and carefully collated by me with the original register. Our hero was their thirteenth child. Patient inquiry has enabled me to verify the following history of their propagations. On July 25, the year after their marriage, Mrs. Ginx was safely delivered of a girl. No announcement of this ap-

peared in the newspapers. On the 10th of April
following, the whole neighborhood, including Great
Smith Street, Marsham Street, Great and Little Peter
Streets, Regent Street, Horseferry Road, and Strutton
Ground, was convulsed by the report that a woman
named Ginx had given birth to "a triplet," consisting
of two girls and a boy. The news penetrated to Dean's
Yard and the ancient school of Westminster. The
dean, who accepted nothing on trust, sent to verify the
report; his messenger bearing a bundle of baby-clothes
from the dean's wife, who thought that the mother
could scarcely have provided for so large an addition to
her family. The schoolboys, on their way to the play-
ground at Vincent Square, slyly diverged to have a look
at the curiosity; paying sixpence a head to Mrs. Ginx's
friend and crony, Mrs. Spittal, who pocketed the money,
and said nothing about it to the sick woman. *This* birth
was announced in all the newspapers throughout the
kingdom, with the further news that her Majesty the
Queen had been graciously pleased to forward to Mrs.
Ginx the sum of three pounds.

What could have possessed the woman, I can't say; but,
about a twelvemonth after, Mrs. Ginx, with the assistance of two doctors hastily fetched from the hospital by
her frightened husband, nearly perished in a fresh effort
of maternity. This time, two sons and two daughters
fell to the lot of the happy pair. Her Majesty sent four
pounds. But, whatever peace there was at home, broils
disturbed the street. The neighbors, who had sent for
the police on the occasion, were angered by a notoriety
which was becoming uncomfortable to them, and began
to testify their feelings in various rough ways. Ginx

removed his family to Rosemary Street, where, up to a year before the time when Ginx's Baby was born, his wife had continued to add to her offspring until the tale reached one dozen. It was then that Ginx affectionately but firmly begged that his wife would consider her family ways, since, in all conscience, he had fairly earned the blessedness of " the man who hath his quiver full of them ; " and frankly gave her notice, that as his utmost efforts could scarcely maintain their existing family, if she ventured to present him with any more, either single or twins or triplets or otherwise, he would most assuredly drown him or her or them in the water-butt, and take the consequences.

II. — HOME, SWEET HOME.

THE day on which Ginx uttered his awful threat was that next to the one wherein number twelve had drawn his first breath. His wife lay on the bed, which, at the outset of wedded life, they had purchased second-hand in Strutton Ground for the sum of nine shillings and sixpence. *Second-hand !* — it had passed through, at least, as many hands as there were afterwards babies born upon it : twelfth or thirteenth hand, a vagabond, botched bedstead, type of all the furniture in Ginx's rooms and in numberless houses through the vast city. Its dimensions were four feet six inches by six feet. When Ginx, who was a stout navvy, and Mrs. Ginx, who was, you may conceive, a matronly woman, were in it, there was little vacant space about them. Yet, as they were forced to find resting-places for all the children, it not

seldom happened that at least one infant was perilously
wedged between the parental bodies; and, latterly, they
had been so pressed for room in the household, that two
younglings were nestled at the foot of the bed.   Without foot-boards or pillows, the lodgement of these infants
was precarious, since any fatuous movement of Ginx's
legs was likely to expel them head first.   However, they
were safe; for they were sure to fall on one or other of
their brothers or sisters.

I shall be as particular as a valuer, and describe what
I have seen. [The family sleeping-room measured thirteen feet six inches by fourteen feet. Opening out of
this, and again on the landing of the third floor, was
their kitchen and sitting-room : it was not quite so large
as the other.   This room contained a press, an old chest
of drawers, a wooden box (once used for navvy's tools),
three chairs, a stool, and some cooking-utensils.   When,
therefore, one little Ginx had curled himself up under a
blanket on the box, and three more had slipped beneath
a tattered piece of carpet under the table, there still remained five little bodies to be bedded.   For them, an
old straw-mattress, limp enough to be rolled up and
thrust under the bed, was at night extended on the floor.]
With this, and a patchwork-quilt, the five were left to
pack themselves together as best they could : so that
if Ginx, in some vision of the night, happened to be angered, and struck out his legs in navvy fashion, it sometimes came to pass that a couple of children tumbled
upon the mass of infantile humanity below.

Not to be described are the dinginess of the walls,
the smokiness of the ceilings, the grimy windows, the
heavy, ever-murky atmosphere of these rooms.   They

were eight feet six inches in height; and any curious statist can calculate the number of cubic feet of air which they afforded to each person.

The other side of the street was fourteen feet distant. Behind, the backs of similar tenements came up black and cowering over the little yard of Number Five. As rare, in the well thus formed, was the circulation of air as that of coin in the pockets of the inhabitants.] I have seen the yard: let me warn you, if you are fastidious, not to enter it. [Such of the filth of the house as could not at night be thrown out of the front-windows was there collected, and seldom, if ever, removed. What became of it? What becomes of countless such accretions in like places? Is a large proportion of these filthy atoms absorbed by human creatures living and dying, instead of being carried away by scavengers and inspectors? The forty-five big and little lodgers in the house were provided with a single office in the corner of the yard. It had once been capped by a cistern, long since rotted away.

．　．　．　．　．　．　．　．　．　．

The street was at one time the prey of the gas company; at another, of the drainage contractors. They seemed to delight in turning up the fetid soil, cutting deep trenches through various strata of filth, and piling up for days or weeks matter that reeked with vegetable and animal decay.] One needs not affirm that Rosemary Street was not so called from its fragrance. If the Ginxes and their neighbors preserved any semblance of health in this place, the most popular guardian on the board must own it a miracle. They, poor people, knew nothing of "sanitary reform," "sanitary precautions," "zymotics," "endemics," "epidemics," "deodorizers," or "disinfectants." They regarded disease with the apathy of creatures who felt it to be inseparable from humanity, and with the fatalism of despair.

Gin was their cardinal prescription, not for cure, but for oblivion: "Sold everywhere." A score of palaces flourished within call of each other in that dismal district, — garish, rich-looking dens, drawing to the support of their vulgar glory the means, the lives, the eternal destinies, of the wrecked masses about them. Veritable wreckers they who construct these haunts, viler than the wretches who place false beacons and plunder bodies on the beach. Bring down the real owners of these places, and show them their deadly work! — some of them leading philanthropists, eloquent at missionary meetings and Bible societies, paying tribute to the Lord out of the pockets of dying drunkards, fighting glorious battles for slaves, and manfully upholding popular rights. My rich publican, — forgive the pun, — before you pay tithes of mint and cumin, much more before you claim to be a disciple of a certain Nazarene, take a lesson from one who restored fourfold the money he had wrung from honest toil, or reflect on the case of the man to whom it was said, " Go sell all thou hast, and give to the poor." The lips from which that counsel dropped offered some unpleasant alternatives; leaving out one, however, which nowadays may yet reach you, — the contempt of your kind.

III. — WORK AND IDEAS.

I RETURN again to Ginx's menace to his wife, who was suckling her infant at the time on the bed. For her he had an animal affection, that preserved her from unkindness, even in his cups. His hand had never unmanned itself by striking her; and rarely, indeed, did it injure any one else. He wrestled not against flesh and blood, or powers or principalities, or wicked spirits in high places : he struggled with clods and stones and primeval chaos. His hands were horny with the fight; and his nature had perhaps caught some of the dull ruggedness of the things wherewith he battled. Hard and with a will had he worked through the years of wedded life ; and, to speak him fair, he had acted honestly, within the limits of his knowledge and means, for the good of his family. How narrow were those limits! Every week he threw into the lap of Mrs. Ginx the eighteen or twenty shillings which his strength and temperance enabled him continuously to earn, less sixpence reserved for the public-house, whither he retreated on Sundays after the family dinner. A dozen children, over-running the space in his rooms, was then a strain beyond the endurance of Ginx. Nor had he the heart to try the common plan, and turn his children out of doors, on the chance of their being picked up in a raid of Sunday-school teachers. So he turned out himself to talk with the humbler spirits of " The Dragon," or listen sleepily while alehouse demagogues prescribed remedies for State abuses.

Our friend was nearly as guiltless of knowledge as if Eve had never rifled the tree whereon it grew. Vacant

of policies were his thoughts; innocent he of ideas of
State-craft.   He knew there was a Queen : he had seen
her.   Lords and Commons were to him vague deities
possessing strange powers : indeed, he had been present
when some of his better-informed companions had recognized with cheers certain gentlemen — of whom Ginx's
estimate was expressed by a reference to his test of su-
periority to himself in that which he felt to be greatest
within him, " I could lick 'em with my little finger ! " —
as the chancellor of the exchequer and the prime-minister.   Little recked he of their uses or abuses.   The
functions of government were to him Asian mysteries.
He only felt that it ought to have a strong arm, like the
brawny member wherewith he preserved order in his
domestic kingdom ; and therefore generally associated
government with the police.   In his view, these were
to clear away evil-doers, and leave every one else alone.
The higher objects of government were, if at all, outlined in the shadowiest form in his imagination.   Government imposed taxes : that he was obliged to know.
Government maintained the parks : for that he thanked
it.   Government made laws ; but what they were, or
with what aim or effects made, he knew not, save only
that by them something was done to raise or depress the
prices of bread, tea, sugar, and other necessaries.   Why
they should do so, he never conceived : I am not sure
that he cared.   Legislation sometimes pinched him ; but
darkness so hid from him the persons and objects of the
legislators, that he could not criticise the theories which
those powerful beings were subjecting to experiment at
his cost.   I must, at any risk, say something about this
in a separate chapter.

IV. — Digressive, and may be skipped without mutilating the History.

I stop here to address any of the following characters, should he perchance read these memoirs : —

You, Mr. Statesman, — if there be such ;

    Mr. Pseudo - Statesman, Placeman, Party - Leader, Wire-Puller ;

    Mr. Amateur Statesman, Dilettante Lord, Civil Servant ;

    Mr. Clubman, Littérateur, Newspaper Scribe ;

    Mr. People's Candidate, Demagogue, Fenian Spouter, —

or whoever you may be, professing to know aught or do any thing in matters of policy, consider, what I am sure you have never fairly weighed, the condition of a man whose clearest notion of government is derived from the police. Imagine one, who had never seen a polype, trying to construct an ideal of the animal from a single tentacle swinging out from the tangle of weed in which the rest was wrapped! How, then, any more can you fancy that a man, to whose sight and knowledge the only part of government practically exposed is the strong process of police, shall form a proper conception of the functions, reasons, operations, and relations of government, or even build up an ideal of any thing but a haughty, unreasonable, antagonistic, tax-imposing FORCE? And how can you rule such a being except as you rule a dog, by that which alone he understands, — the dog-whip of the constable? Given in a country a majority of creatures like these, and surely despotism is its properest complement. But when they exist, as they exist in

England to-day, in hundreds of thousands, in town and country, think what a complication they introduce into your theoretic free system of government. Acts of Parliament passed by a "freely-elected" House of Commons and an hereditary House of Lords, under the threats of freely-electing citizens, however pure in intention and correct in principle, will not seem to him to be the resultants of every wish in the community so much as dictations by superior strength. To these the obedience he will render will not be the loving assent of his heart, but a begrudged concession to circumstance. Your awe-invested legislature is not viewed as his friend and brother-helper, but his tyrant. Therefore the most natural bent of his workman-statesmanship — a rough, bungling affair — will be to tame you, — you who ought to be his counsellor and friend. When he finds that your legislative action exerts upon him a repressive and restraining force, he will curse you as its author, because he sees not the springs you are working. Should he even be a little more advanced in knowledge than our friend Ginx, and learn that he helps to elect the Parliament to make laws on behalf of himself and his fellow-citizens, he will scarce trust the assembly which is supposed to represent him. Will he, like a good citizen and a politic, accept with dignity and self-control the decision of a majority against his prejudices ? or will he not regard the whole Wittenagemote with suspicion, contempt, or even hatred ? See him rush madly to Trafalgar-square meetings, Hyde-park demonstrations, perhaps to Lord George Gordon riots, as if there were no less perilous means of publishing his opinions ! There wily men may lead his unconscious intellect, and stir his passions, and direct his forces against his own and his children's good.

Did it ever occur to you, or any of you, how many voters cannot read, and how many more, though they can read, are unable to apprehend reasons of statesmanship? that even newspapers cannot inform them, since they have not the elementary knowledge needed for the comprehension of those things which are discussed in them? nay, that, for want of understanding the same, they may terribly distort political aims and consequences?

Might it not be worth while for you, gentlemen, may it not be your duty, to devise ways and means for conveying such elementary instruction by good street-preachers on politics and economy, or even political Bible-women or colporters, and so to make clear to the understanding of every voter what are the reasons and aims of every act of legislation, home administration, and foreign policy? If you do not find out some way to do this, he may turn round upon you, — I hope he may, — and insist on annually-elected parliaments, and thus oblige ambitious State-mongers, in the rivalry of place, to come to him and declare more often their wishes and objects. Other attractions may be found in that solution; such as the untying of some knots of electoral difficulty, and removing incitements to corruption. Ten thousand pounds for one year's power were a high price, even to a contractor. Think, then, whether, at any cost, some general political education must not be attempted, since there is a spirit breathing on the waters; and how it shall convulse them is no indifferent matter to you or to me. Everywhere around us are unhewn rocks stirred with a strange motion. Leave these chaotic fragments

of humanity to be hewn into rough shape by coarse
artists seeking only a petty profit, unhandy, immeasura-
bly impudent; or dress them by your teaching — teaching which is the highest, noblest, purest, most efficient
function of government, which ought to be the most lofty
ambition of statesmanship — to be civic corner-stones,
polished after the similitude of a palace.

V. — REASONS AND RESOLVES.

GINX has been waiting through three chapters to
explain his truculence upon the birth of his twelfth
child. Much explanation is not necessary. When he
looked round his nest and saw the many open mouths
about him, he might well be appalled to have another
added to them. His children were not chameleons: yet
they were already forced to be content with a proportion
of air for their food; and even the air was bad. They
were pallid and pinched. How they were clad will ever
be a mystery, save to the poor woman who strung the
limp rags together, and Him who watched the noble pa-
tience and sacrifice of a daily heroism. Of her own
unsatisfied cravings, and the dense motherly horrors
that sometimes brooded over her while she nursed these
infants, let me refrain from speaking; since, if as vividly
depicted as they were real, you, madam, could not endure
to read of them. Her poor, unintelligent mind clung
tenaciously to the controverted aphorism, "Where God
sends mouths, he sends food to fill them." Believing
that there was a God, and that he must be kind, she
trusted in this as a truth: and perhaps an all-seeing Eye,
reading some quaint characters on her simple heart,

viewed them not too nearly, but had regard to their general import; for, as she expressed it, "Thank God! they had always been able to get along."

In the rush and tumult of the world, it is likely that the *summum bonum* of nine-tenths of mankind is embraced in that purely negative happiness,—to get along; not to perish; to open eyes, however wearily, on a new morning; to satisfy with something, no matter what, a craving appetite; to close eyes at night under some shadow or shelter; or, it may be, in certain ranks to walk another day free from bankruptcy or arrest. Thank Heaven! they are just able to get along.

Convinced that another infant straw would break his back, Ginx calmly proposed to disconcert physical, moral, and legal relations by drowning the straw. Mrs. Ginx, clinging to Number Twelve, listened aghast. If a mother can forget her sucking child, she was not that mother. The stream of her affections, though divided into twelve rills, would not have been exhausted in twenty-four; and her soul, forecasting its sorrow, yearned after that nonentity, Number Thirteen. She pictured to herself the hapless strangeling borne away from her bosom by those strong arms; and, in fact, she sobbed so, that Ginx grew ashamed, and sought to comfort her by the suggestior that she could not have any more. But she knew better.

———◆———

VI.—THE ANTAGONISM OF LAW AND NECESSITY.

IN eighteen months, notwithstanding resolves, menaces, and prophecies, GINX'S BABY was born. The mother hid the impending event long from the father.

When he came to know it, he fixed his determination by much thought and a little extra drinking. He argued thus: "He wouldn't go on the parish. He couldn't keep another youngster to save his life. He had never taken charity, and never would. There was nothink to do with it but drown it!" Female friends of Mrs. Ginx bruited his intentions about the neighborhood, so that her "time" was watched for with interest. At last it came. One afternoon, Ginx, lounging home, saw signs of excitement around his door in Rosemary Street. A knot of women and children awaited his coming. Passing through them, he soon learned what had happened. Poor Mrs. Ginx! Without staying to think or argue, he took up the little stranger, and bore it from the room ——

"Oh, oh, oh! Ginx! Ginx!"

She would have risen; but a strong power, called weakness, pulled her back.

. . . .

The man meanwhile had reached the street.

"Here he comes! There's the baby! He's going to do it, sure enough!" shrieked the women. The children stood agape. He stopped to consider. It is very well to talk about drowning your baby; but to do it you need two things, — water and opportunity. Vauxhall Bridge was the nearest way to the former; and towards it Ginx turned.

"Stop him!"

"Murder!"

"Take the child from him!"

The crowd grew larger, and impeded the man's progress. Some of his fellow-workmen stood by regarding the fun.

"Leave us aloan, naabors!" shouted Ginx: "this is my own baby, and I'll do wot I likes with it. I kent keep it; an,' if I've got any thin' I kent keep, it's best to get rid of it, ain't it? This child's goin' over Wauxhall Bridge."

But the women clung to his arms and coat-tails.

"Hallo! what's all this about?" said a sharp, strong man, well dressed, and in good condition, coming up to the crowd, — "another foundling? Confound the place! the very stones produce babies! Where was it found?"

CHORUS (*recognizing a deputy-relieving officer*). It warn't found at all: it's Ginx's baby.

OFFICER. — Ginx's baby? Who's Ginx?

GINX. — I am.

OFFICER. — Well?

GINX. — Well!

CHORUS. — He's goin' to drown it.

OFFICER. — Going to drown it? Nonsense!

GINX. — I am.

OFFICER. — But, bless my heart, that's murder!

GINX. — No 'tain't. I've twelve already at home. Starvashon's sure to kill this 'un. Best save it the trouble.

CHORUS. — Take it away, Mr. Smug: he'll kill it if you don't.

OFFICER. — Stuff and nonsense! Quite contrary to law! Why, man, you're bound to support your child. You can't throw it off in that way; nor on the parish neither. Give me your name. I must get a magistrate's order. The act of Parliament is as clear as daylight. I had a man up under it last week. "Whosoever shall unlawfully abandon or expose any child being under the age of two years whereby the life of such child shall be endangered or the health of such child shall have been or shall be likely to be permanently injured (drowning comes under that I think) shall be *guilty of a* MISDE-MEANOR and being convicted thereof shall be liable at the discretion of the court to be *kept in* PENAL SERVI-TUDE for the term of three years or to be imprisoned for any term not exceeding two years with or without hard labor."

Mr. Smug the officer rolled out this section in a sonorous monotone, without stops, like a clerk of the court. It was his pride to know by heart all the acts relating to his department, and to bring them down upon any obstinate head that he wished to crush. Ginx's head, however, was impervious to an act of Parliament. In his then temper, the commination-service or St. Ernulphus's curse would have been feathers to him. The only feeling aroused in his mind by the words of the legislature was one of resentment. To him they seemed unjust because they were hard and fast, and made no allowance for circumstances. So he said, —

GINX. — D—— the act of Parliament! What's the use of saying I sha'n't abandon the child, when I can't keep it alive?

OFFICER. — But you're bound by law to keep it alive.

GINX. — Bound to keep it alive? How am I to do it? There's the rest on 'em there (nodding towards his house) little better nor alive now. If that's an act of Parleyment, why don't the act of Parleyment provide for 'em? You know what wages is; and I can't get more than is going.

CHORUS. — Yes. Why don't Parleyment provide for 'em ? You take the child, Mr. Smug.

OFFICER (*regardless of grammar*). — *Me* take the child! The parish has enough to do to take care of foundlings, and children whose parents can't or don't work. You don't suppose we will look after the children of those who can ?

GINX. — Jest so. You'll bring up bastards and beggars' pups; but you won't help an honest man to keep his head above water. This child's head is goin' under water anyhow! And he prepared to bolt, amid fresh screams from the chorus.

VII. — MALTHUS AND MAN.

Two gentlemen who had been observing the excitement here came forward.

FIRST GENTLEMAN. — This is our problem again, Mr. Philosopher.

MR. PHILOSOPHER (*to Ginx*). — You don't know what to do with your infant, my friend ; and you think the State ought to provide for it ? I understand you to say this is your thirteenth child. How came you to have so many ?

This question, though put with profound and even melancholy gravity, disconcerted Ginx, Officer, and Chorus, who united in a hearty outburst of laughter.

GINX. — Haw, haw, haw ! How came I to have so many? Why, my old woman's a good 'un, and —

In fact, after searching his mind for some clever way

of putting a comical rejoinder, Ginx laughed boisterous·
ly.   There are two aspects of a question.

PHILOSOPHER. — I am serious, my friend. Did it never
occur to you that you had no right to bring children into
the world unless you could feed and clothe and educate
them ?

CHORUS. — Laws a' mercy !

GINX. — I'd like to know how I could help it, naabor.
I'm a married man.

PHILOSOPHER. — Well, I will go further, and say you
ought not to have married without a fair prospect of
being able to provide for any contingent increase of
family.

CHORUS. — Laws a' mercy !

PHILOSOPHER (*waxing warm*).   What right had you
to marry a poor woman, and then both of you, with as
little forethought as two — a — dogs, or other brutes —
to produce between you such a multitudinous progeny ? —

GINX. — Civil words, naabor. Don't call my family
hard names.

PHILOSOPHER. — Then let me say such a monstrous
number of children as thirteen ?   You knew, as you
said just now, that wages were wages, and did not vary
much ; and yet you have gone on subdividing your
resources by the increase of what must become a degen-
erate offspring. (*To the Chorus.*) All you workpeople
are doing it.   Is it not time to think about these things,
and stop the indiscriminate production of human beings
whose lives you cannot properly maintain ?   Ought you
not to act more like reflective creatures, and less like
brutes ?   As if breeding were the whole object of life !
How much better for you, my friend, if you had never

married at all, than to have had the worry of a wife and children all these years !

The philosopher had gone too far. There were some angry murmurs among the women; and Ginx's face grew dark. He was thinking of "all those years," and the poor creature that from morning to night, and Sunday to Sunday, in calm and storm, had clung to his rough affections; and the bright eyes; and the winding arms so often trellised over his tremendous form; and the coy tricks and laughter that had cheered so many tired hours. He may have been much of a brute; but he felt, that, after all, that sort of thing was denied to dogs and pigs. Before he could translate his thoughts into words or acts, a shrewd-looking, curly-haired stonemason, who stood by with his tin on his arm, cut into the discussion.

STONEMASON. — Your doctrines won't go down here, Mr. Philosopher. I've 'eard of them before. I'd just like to ask you what a man's to do, and what a woman's to do, if they don't marry ; and, if they do, how can you honestly hinder them from having any children ?

The stonemason had rudely struck out the cardinal issues of the question.

PHILOSOPHER. — Well, to take the last point first, there are physical and ethical questions involved in it which it is hard to discuss before such an audience as this.

STONEMASON. — But you must discuss 'em, if you wish us to change our ways and stop breeding.

PHILOSOPHER. — Very well: perhaps you are right. But, again, I should first have to establish a basis for my arguments by showing that the conception of marriage entertained by you all is a low one. It is not simply a breeding matter. The beauty and value of the relation lies in its educational effects, — the cultivation of mutual sentiments and refinements of great importance to a community.

STONEMASON. — Ay! Very beautiful and refining to Mr. and Mrs. Philosopher; but I'd like to know where the country would have been if our fathers had held to that view of matrimony? Why, ain't it in natur' for all beings to pair, and have young? an' you say we ain't to do it! I think a statesman ought to make something out of what's nateral to human beings, and not try to change their naturs. Besides, ain't there good of another kind to be got out of the relation of parents and children? Did you ever have a child yourself?

GINX (*contemplating the philosopher's physique*). *He* have a youngster! He couldn't.

CHORUS. — Ha, ha, ha!

STONEMASON. — I don't believe in yer humbuggin' notions. They lead to lust and crime: I'm told they do in France. If you yourself haven't the human natur in you to know it, I'll tell you, and we can all tell you, that, as a rule, if the healthy desires of natur ain't satisfied in a honest way, they will be in another. You can't stop eating by passin' an act of Parleyment to stop it; and, as for yer eddication and cultivation, that makes no difference. We know something here about yer eddicated men, — more than they think. Who is it we meet about the streets late at night goin' to the gay houses? Some of 'em stand near as high as you; but that don't alter their natur. They have their passions like other men; and eddication don't keep 'em down. Well, if that's the case, how can you ask people of our sort to put on the curb, or make us do it? Are we to live more like beasts than we are now, or do what's worse than murder? I don't see no other way. Among us, I tell you, sir, three-fourths of our eddication is eddication of the heart. We have to learn to be human, kind, self-denyin': and I think this makes better men, as a rule, than head-larnin'; though I don't despise that, neither. But you don't suppose head-citizens would fight for their country like men with wives and children behind 'em? Why, they don't even at home work for daily food like a man with wife and babies to provide for.

The stonemason was above his class, — one of those shrewd men that "the people called Methodists" get hold of, and use among the lower orders under the name of "local preachers;" men who learn to think and speak better than their fellows. The philosopher testified some admiration by listening attentively, and was about to reply; but the chorus was tired, and the women would not hear him.

CHORUS. — Best get out o' this. We don't want any o' yer filhosophy. Go and get childer' of yer own, &c.

The philosopher and his friend departed, carrying with them unsolved the problem they had brought.

—◆—

VIII. — THE BABY'S FIRST TRANSLATION.

THE stonemason had been the hero of the moment: now attention centred on our own hero. Ginx hurried off again; but, as the crowd opened before him, he was met, and his mad career stayed, by a slight figure, femi-nine, draped in black to the feet, wearing a curiously-framed white-winged hood above her pale face, and a large cross suspended from her girdle. He could not run her down.

NUN. — Stop, MAN ! Are you mad ? Give me the child.

He placed the little bundle in her arms. She uncovered the queer ruby face, and kissed it. Ginx had not looked at the face before ; but after seeing it, and the act of this woman, he could not have touched a hair of his child's head. His purpose died from that moment, though his perplexity was still alive.

NUN. — Let me have it. I will take it to the Sisters' Home, and it shall live there. Your wife may come and nurse it. We will take charge of it.

GINX. — And you won't send it back again ? You'll take it for good and all ?

NUN. — Oh, yes !

GINX. — Good ! Give us yer hand.

A little white hand came out from under her burthen, and was at once half crushed in Ginx's elephantine grasp.

GINX. — Done. Thank'ee, missus. Come, mates, I'll stand a drink.

A few minutes after, the woman of the cross, who had been up to comfort the poor mother, fluttered with her white wings down Rosemary Street, carrying in her arms Ginx's Baby.

PART II.

WHAT CHARITY AND THE CHURCHES DID WITH HIM.

I. — The Milk of Human Kindness, Mother's Milk, and the Milk of the Word.

THE early days of his residence at the Home of the Sisters of Misery, in Winkle Street, was the Eden of Ginx's Baby's existence. Themselves innocent of a mother's experiences, the Sisters were free to give play to their affections in a novel direction, and to assume a sort of spiritual maternity that was lucky for the changeling. He was nestled in kind serge-covered arms : kisses rained upon him from chaste lips. A slight scandal thrilled the convent upon the discovery of his sex, which had, of course, been a pure matter of conjecture to Sister Pudicitia when she rescued him ; but enthusiasm can overcome any thing. The awkward questions foreshadowed in the discovery were left to be considered when their growing importance should demand upon them the judgment of the archbishop. Visions of an unusual sanctity to be fostered in the pure regions of the convent, and to be sent on a mission into the world to attest the power of their spiritual discipline, began to

35

haunt the brains of the sequestered nuns. Might not this infant be an embryo saint, destined for a great work in the heretical wilderness out of which he had come? How little healthy food the brains must have had wherein these insane dreams were excited by our innocent baby! Hardly did the sacred spinsters forecast what was in store for them when he should be teething.

But Ginx's Baby was in a religious atmosphere, and that is always surcharged with electricity. His lot must have been above that of any other human being if he could long have remained in such a climate unvisited by thunder. The mother had been. permitted to attend at the Home with the same regularity as the milkman, to discharge her maternal duties. Then, with the rise of the visionary projects just mentioned, the gravest doubts began to agitate the fertile and casuistic mind of the lady-superior. The holier her ideal St. Ginx of the future, the more to be deplored was. any heretical taint in the present. Holy Mother! Was it not perhaps eminently perilous to his spiritual purity that an unbeliever like Mrs. Ginx should bring unconsecrated milk into the convent to be administered to this suckling of the Church! In her uneasiness, she appealed to Father Certificatus, the conventual confessor. He gave his opinion in the following letter: —

"DEAR SISTER SUSPICIOSA, — The very grave question you have put to me has given me much anxiety. It could not but do so, since it occupied, I knew, so fully your own holy reflections. I pondered it during the night while I repeated one hundred Aves on my knees; and I think the Blessed Virgin has vouchsafed her assistance.

"I understood you to say you thought that the physical health of the infant, so singularly and miraculously thrown upon your care, required the offices of his heretic mother, and yet that you felt how inconsistent it was, with the noble future we contemplate for him, that he should receive unorthodox lacteal sustentation. In this you are but following the usage of the Church in all ages; for she has ever enjoined the advantage of infusing her doctrines into her children with the mother's milk.

"Three courses only appear to me to be open to us. First, we may try to work upon the mother's feelings, and, on behalf of her child, induce her to avail herself of the inestimable privileges of the Church in which he is fostered. Secondly, should she repel us, — and these lower-class heretics are even brutally refractory, — we might at least allure her to allow us to make with holy water the sign of the cross upon the natural reservoirs of infant nourishment each time before she approaches the infant. This, besides overcoming the immediate difficulty, and securing for the child a supply of sanctified food, might open the way for the entrance into her own bosom of the milk of the Word. Thirdly, should she reject these proposals, I see nothing for it but to forbid her to have access to her infant, and, commending him to the care of the Holy Mother, to feed him with pap or other suitable nourishment previously consecrated by me in its crude state, and prepared by the most holy hands of your community. Thus we may hope to shield the young soul in its present freshness from contact with carnal elements.

"Your loving father in, &c.,

"CERTIFICATUS."

On receiving this letter, the superioress conferred not with flesh and blood, but sent for Mrs. Ginx. That worthy woman was not enchanted with her child's position. I have hinted that her faith was simple; but, in proportion to its simplicity, it was strongly rooted in her nature. 'Tis not infrequent to find it so. Lengthy creeds, and confessions of faith, are apt to extend the strength and fervor of belief over too wide a surface: in the close frame of some single article will be concentrated the whole energy of the soul. The first formula, " Repent, and believe in the Lord Jesus Christ," was maintained with a heat that became less intense, though more distributed, in the insertion of an Athanasian Creed. Mrs. Ginx's creed was succinct.

Mrs. Ginx's Primary Creed.

I believe in God, giver of bread, meat, money, and health.

This she maintained with indifferent ritual and devotional observances. But there was to Mrs. Ginx's faith a corollary or secondary creed, only needed to meet special emergencies.

Mrs. Ginx's Secondary Creed.

1. I believe in the Church of England.
2. I believe in heaven and hell.
3. (A negative article) I hate Popery, priests, and the Devil.

When her husband made his fatal gift to the nun,

this third article of his wife's belief, or unbelief, stirred up, and waxed aggressive.

Said the lady-superior, "My good woman, your child thrives under the care of Holy Mother Church."

"Yes'm, he thrives well," replies Mrs. Ginx, repeating no more of Sister Suspiciosa's sentence; "an' I've 'ad more milk than ever for the darlin' this time, thank God!"

"And the Holy Virgin."

"I dunno about her," cries Mrs. Ginx emphatically, perhaps not seeing congruity between a virgin and the subject of thankfulness.

"And the Holy Virgin," repeated the nun, "who interests herself in all mothers. She has thus blessed you, that your child may be made strong for the work of the Church. Do you not see a miracle is worked within you to prove her goodness? This, no doubt, is an evidence to you of her wish to bless you, and take you for her own. I beseech you, listen to her voice, and come and enter her fold."

"If you mean the Virgin Mary, mum, I ain't a idolater, beggin' yer parding," says Mrs. Ginx. "An' tho' I wouldn't for the world offend them as has been so kind to my child, an' saved it from that deer little creetur bein' thrown over Wauxhall Bridge, — an' Ginx ought to be ashamed of hisself, so he ought, — I ain't Papish, mum; and I ain't dispoged, with twelve on 'em there at home, all Protestant to the back-bone, to turn Papish now: an' so I 'ope an' pray, mum," says Mrs. Ginx, roaring and crying, "you ain't agoin' to make Papish of my flesh an' blood. Oh, dear! oh, dear!"

The lady-superior shut her ears: she had raised a familiar spirit, and could not lay it. She temporized.

" You know your husband has given the child to us.
It will be called the infant Ambrosius."

" Dear, dear ! " sighed Mrs. Ginx : " what a name ! "

" We wish him to be kept from any worldly taint ;
and by and by his saintliness may gain you forgiveness
in spite of your heretical perversity. I cannot permit
you to give him unconsecrated milk ; and, as we wish to
treat you kindly, the holy Father Certificatus has allowed me to make an arrangement with you, to which
you can have no objection, — I mean, that you should let
me make the sign of the cross upon your breasts, morning and evening, before you suckle your infant. You
will permit me to do that, won't you ? "

Conceive of Mrs. Ginx's reply, clothed in choice Westminster English ! It asserted her readiness to cut off her
right hand, her feet, to be hanged, drowned, burned,
torn to pieces, in fact to withstand all the torments as-
cribed by vulgar tradition to Roman-Catholic ingenuity,
and to see her baby " a dead corpse " into the bargain,
before she would submit her Protestant bosom to such
an indignity.

" No, mum ! " she said : "I couldn't sleep with that on
my breast ; " and cried hysterically.

This lower-class heretic *was* " brutally refractory."
So thought the superioress, and so gave Mrs. Ginx notice to come no more. She went home rather jubilant :
she was a martyr.

II. — The Protestant Detectoral Association.

GINX'S BABY was now fed on consecrated pap. But his mother was not a woman to be silent under her wrongs. From her husband she hid them, because the subject was forbidden. She poured out her complaint to Mrs. Spittal and other Protestant matrons. Thus it came to pass, that one day, in Ginx's absence, the good woman was surprised by a visit from a " gentleman." He was small, sharp, rapid, dressed in black. He opened his business at once.

" Mrs. Ginx ? Ah ! I am the agent of the Protestant Detectoral Association."

Mrs. Ginx wiped her best chair, and set it for him.

" By great good fortune, the secretary received only half an hour ago intelligence of the shocking instance of Papal aggression of which you have been the victim."

To hear her case put so grandly was honey to Mrs. Ginx.

" Well, now," continued the little man, " we are ready to render you every assistance to save your child from the claws of the Great Dragon. I wish to know the exact circumstances. Let me see (opening a large pocket-book), I have this memorandum : *The child was carried off from his mother's bedside in broad daylight by a nun, accompanied by two priests and a large body of Irish :* is that a correct version ? "

" Law, no, sir ! it warn't quite like that," said Mrs. Ginx. " We've 'ad so many on 'em, that Ginx was for drownin' the thirteenth," — the little man opened his eyes, —

"An' he went and gave it away, sir," said she, crying, "to a nun, sir, — ah, ah, ah! They won't let me see the darlin' now, sir, — ah, ah, ah! because I won't let Missis Spishyosir mark me with the cross, sir; an' me with as fine a breast o' milk as ever was for 'im, sir, — ah, ah, ah!"

"Hem!" said the little man : "that's different from what I understood."

He was quite honest; but who does not know how disappointing it is to find a wrong you wish to redress is not so bad as you had hoped?

However, it looked bad enough, and might be made worse. It was the very case for the Protestant Detectoral Association.

"Would Mr. Ginx not join in an effort to recover his child?"

"No, sir : I should think not. He went an' gave it away."

"I know; but he is a Protestant?"

"I don't think he be much o' any thing, sir. I know he hate priests like pison; but he don't care about these things as I do."

"Oh! I see." Writes in his memorandum-book, — *Husband indifferent.*

"But don't you think he would help you to get the child back again?"

"No, sir! I wouldn't speak of it to him for the world. He'd knock any one down if they was to mention the child to him."

The little man mentally determined not to see Ginx.

"Well : would you like to have your child back?"

"You see, I couldn't bring it 'ere, sir. Ginx won't

'ave it; but I'd like to see it took away from them nun-
neries."

"Ha! very well, then. We can perhaps manage it
for you. You would be content to hand it over to some
Protestant Home, where it would be taken care of, and
you could see it when you liked?"

"Oh, yes, sir!" cries Mrs. Ginx, brightening.

"Then we'll have an affidavit, and apply for a *habeas
corpus.*"

It was impossible not to be satisfied with such words
as these, whatever they meant; and Mrs. Ginx was
cheered, while the little man went on his way.

———◆———

III.—THE SACRAMENT OF BAPTISM.

MOTHER, or "MRS." SUSPICIOSA, fed Ginx's Baby
with holy pap. It seemed proper, now, that he should
oe christened, and formally received into the Church.
No small stir was made by this ceremony, for which all
the resources of the convent were called into action.
The day selected was that sacred to St. Ambrosius. The
chapel was decorated with flowers; mass was celebrated;
candles flamed upon the altar surrounding a figure of
the infant Jesus; incense was burning around the baby;
sisters and novices knelt in serried rows of virginity

> "Like doves
> Sunning their milky bosoms on the thatch."

Mother Suspiciosa carried the infant clothed in a pure
white robe with a red cross embroidered on its front.

In the absence of the natural parent, a wax figure of St. Ambrosius did duty for him, and another wax figure stood godfather. But I dare not enter into details of matters that may be looked at as awfully profane or awfully solemn by different spectators. These things are a mystery.

I have no hesitation about describing the impious behavior of little Ginx. Whatever swaddled infant could do in the way of opposition, with hands and legs and voice, was done by that embryo saint. The incense made him cough and sputter : the lights and singing raised the very devil within him. His cries drowned the prayers. He frightened his conductress by the redness of his face. He ruined the red cross with ejected matter. You would have taken him for an infant demoniac. Mother Suspiciosa, though annoyed, was encouraged. She looked upon this as an evident testimony to little Ginx's value. The Devil and St. Michael were contending for his body. At length he was baptized, and carried out. *Credat Judæus.* He instantly sank into a deep sleep. It was a miracle : Satan had yielded to the sign of the cross !

----◆----

IV.—LAW ON BEHALF OF GOSPEL.

IN the moment of Sister Suspiciosa's triumph, the enemy was laying his train against her. The little man made his report to the secretary of the Protestant Detectoral Association. This gentleman was well born and well bred; moved to work in this "cause" by an honest hatred of superstition, priestcraft, and lies; now giving

all his energies to the ambitious design of pulling down
the strongholds of Satan. In any other matter, he could
act coolly and with deliberation: in this he was an enthusiast. He had a keen Roman nose. He could scent
a priest anywhere in the United Kingdom. He could
smell Jesuitry in the queen's drawing-room, a cabinet
council or convocation, though he had never been at
either. His eye was beyond a falcon's: he saw things
that were invisible. It penetrated through all disguises.
He knew a secret emissary of the pope by the cock of
his hat or the color of his stockings; at least, he
thought so: and thousands of persons acted on his estimate of himself.

"This case," said he to the little man when he had
concluded his report, "though not in its first incidents
so grave as we were led to expect, is, in another point
of view, very serious. Here is a man, as you have expressed it, 'indifferent' to his child's life, animal and
spiritual. The mother, with a true Protestant heart
and a fine breast of milk, is longing to nurture her child,
and to deliver it from the toils of the Papacy. But the
husband, what's his name? . . . Ginx, Ginx? a very
bad name for a case, by the way, — *Ginx's Case!* — this
Ginx has given up his child to the Sisters of Misery.
How are we to get it away again without his co-opera-
tion? . . . Well, we must try."

The solicitor of the association was forthwith summoned. When the matter had been laid before him, he
expressed doubts, offered and withdrew courses of action,
and ended by suggesting that he should take the opinion
of counsel. .

"Mr. Stigma, I suppose?" said he to the secretary.

" Oh, yes ! Sir Adolphus Stigma is one of our principal supporters ; and his son's heart is thoroughly with us."

Messrs. Roundhead, Roundhead and Lollard, drew up a case to be submitted to Mr. Stigma. I will only transcribe the latter paragraphs : —

"*Mr. Ginx being indifferent, and Mrs. Ginx being ready to assist in regaining the custody of her child, to be conveyed to a Protestant Home, —*

" You are Requested to Advise, —

" 1. *Whether a summons should be taken out before a magistrate against the lady-superior of the convent for enticing away or detaining the infant under the 56th sect. of 24 and 25 Vict., c. 100 ; or, —*

" 2. *Whether the proper remedy is by a writ of habeas corpus? and, if so, whether it is necessary that the father should be joined in the proceedings, or his leave obtained to prosecute them ; or, failing these, —*

" 3. *Whether counsel is of opinion that this is a case within Talfourd's Act, and an application might not be made to the Lord Chancellor, or the Master of the Rolls, on the mother's behalf, for the custody of her child ; and, —*

" 4. *To advise generally on behalf of the infant.*"

Mr. Adolphus Stigma took ten days to consider. Meanwhile, the infant Ambrosius continued to thrive on conventual pap. Then Mr. Stigma wrote his opinion. It was a model for a barrister. You took the advice at your own peril, not his : therefore I transcribe it.

" Opinion.

" I have given to this case my most careful attention; and it is one of great difficulty. Having regard to the questions put to me, I think, —

" 1. Section 56 of the Act of 24 and 25 Vict., c. 100, appears at first sight to be directed against the stealing and abduction of children for marriage, or other improper purposes. It provides, that ' whosoever shall *unlawfully*, either by force or fraud, lead or take away or decoy or entice away or detain any child, &c., with intent to deprive *any* parent, &c., of the possession of such child,' shall be guilty of felony. It is perfectly clear, that, in the case before me, the infant was not, ' by force or fraud, led or taken away or decoyed or enticed away.' The statute, however, uses the word ' detain ; ' and this, it appears to me, has much the same force and intention as the previous words. It is to be noted, however, that it is separated from them by the disjunctive ' or ; ' and therefore it might be argued, with some plausibility, that any act of forceful or fraudulent detention, after notice, by persons who have originally acquired a child's custody in a lawful way, came within the section. The point is new, and of great importance ; and, if the Protestant Detectoral Association feel disposed to try it, they would do so under favorable circumstances in the present case. Should they decide to do so, a written demand should be served upon the authorities of the convent by the mother, or some one acting on her behalf, to give up the infant.

" 2. The second question is also involved in difficulty. Were the father to be joined in the proceedings, the writ of *habeas corpus* would be the correct remedy.

But his probable refusal necessitates the inquiry, whether the mother can alone apply for the writ. The general rule of law is, that the father is entitled to the custody and disposition of his children. In *Cartlidge and Cartlidge*, 31 L. J., P. M. & D. 85, it was held that this rule would not be generally departed from by the Divorce Court; but in *Barnes v. Barnes*, L. R. 1, P. & D. 463, the Court made an order, giving the custody of two infant children to the mother, respondent in a suit for a dissolution of marriage, on the ground that the mother's health was suffering from being deprived of their society, and that they were living with a stranger, and not with the father. These cases were, however, in the Divorce Court, and do not apply. But as there seems to be much ground in the peculiar circumstances here for arguing that the mother should have the custody of the child, or, at least, that it should not be left to that of persons of a different religion from both parents, an application might be made to the Queen's Bench to try the question.

" 3. Should the common-law remedies fail, resort may perhaps be had to the powers in Chancery under Talfourd's Act; but on this point I should like to confer with an equity counsel before giving a decided opinion. It has been decided under this act that the Court has power to give the custody of children under seven to the mother (*Shillito v. Collett*, 8, W. R. 683–696). As this infant is but six weeks old, it comes within that case.

" 4. I have no general advice to give on behalf of the infant.

" ADOLPHUS STIGMA,

" *9 Plumtree Court.*"

If none of the courses suggested by Mr. Stigma was very decided, Messrs. Roundhead, Roundhead and Lollard, were not sorry to have three strings to their bow. The Detectoral Association were good clients: most of their funds went into their lawyers' pockets. It was part of their policy to be litigious : thereby the world was kept alive to the existence of Papacy within its bosom. Who shall say the association were wrong? Some healthy daylight was occasionally let in upon the mysteries of Jesuitism ; and there are people who think that worth while at the risk of a chance injustice. Though the Devil should not get his due, few would give him any sympathy.

The solicitor at once instructed Mr. Dignam Bailey, Q.C., to apply with Mr. Stigma to a magistrate for a summons. Mr. Bailey, Q.C., was not chosen for his partialities. In religious matters he was a perfect Gallio : but he was like St. Paul in one particular, — he could be all things to all men.

———◆———

V. — MAGISTRATE'S LAW.

THE personnel of the magistrate to whom Mr. Dignam Bailey, Q. C. (with him Mr. Adolphus Stigma), applied in the case of re an infant, ex parte Ginx, is not material to this history. He was like his fellow stipendiaries, — mild as to humor, vigilant in his duties, opinionated in his views, resenting the troublesome intrusion into his court of a barrister, apt to treat him with about one-eighth of the courtesy extended to the humblest junior by the Queen's Bench, and curiously unequal

4

both with himself and his brother-magistrates in adjust-
ing punishment.   It will be most convenient to insert
the report of " The Daily Electric Meteor : " —

" WESTMINSTER.

"Mr. Dignam Bailey, Q. C. (with whom was Mr.
Adolphus Stigma), applied for a summons against Mary
Dens, commonly called Sister Suspiciosa, of the convent
of the Sisters of Misery, in Winkle Street, for abducting
and detaining a male child of John Ginx, and Mary
his wife.

"MR. D'ACERBITY. — On whose behalf do you apply ?

" The learned counsel stated that he was instructed
by the Protestant Detectoral Association to apply on
behalf of the mother.   The case was also watched by
the solicitors of the Society for preventing the Suppres-
sion of Women and Children.

"MR. D'ACERBITY. — Does the father join in the
application ?

"MR. BAILEY. — No, sir.

"MR. D'ACERBITY. — Why ?   He ought to be joined,
if living.

"MR. BAILEY. — Perhaps you will allow me, sir, to
state the case.   The circumstances are peculiar.   The
fact is —

"MR. D'ACERBITY. — I cannot understand why the
father should not be represented if the child has been
abducted.   Where was it taken from ?

"Mr. Bailey proceeded to state that the child had
been taken by a nun from No. 5, Rosemary Street,
without the mother's consent, and was now imprisoned

in the convent. The father appeared to be indifferent, or to have given a sort of general acquiescence. This was Mrs. Ginx's thirteenth child, around whom gathered the concentrated affections —

"MR. D'ACERBITY (*interrupting the learned gentleman*). We have no time for sentiment here, Mr. Bailey. If the father consented, can you call it abduction? It looks like reduction. (*Laughter.*)

"Mr. Bailey called attention to the consolidated statutes of criminal law, and said he was going for illegal detention rather than abduction, and argued at great length from section fifty-six. At the conclusion of the argument, after refusing to hear Mr. Stigma,

"Mr. D'Acerbity said that the case clearly did not come within the section, and he was afraid the learned counsel knew it. The father had been a consenting party, on the counsel's own statement, to the child's removal; and no suggestion had been made that he had withdrawn his consent. He should refuse a summons.

"Mr. Bailey endeavored to address the magistrate, but was stopped.

"MR. D'ACERBITY. — I have no more to say. You can apply to the Queen's Bench. I have no sympathy with you whatever."

Mr. D'Acerbity's law was good; but what has justice to do with "sympathies"? Surely, the day after this report appeared, the magistrate must have had a letter from the Home Secretary.

VI.—Popery and Protestantism in the Queen's Bench.

The application to the magistrate was far from satisfactory. There had not even been an exposure; and "The Windmill Bulletin" gayly bantered the Detectoral Association. Meanwhile had happened the grand christening, of which a circumstantial account was in the hands of the council of the Detectoral Association shortly after the ceremony had been performed. Here was a monstrous indignity to a Protestant child. The account was at once printed, together with a verbatim report of the application to the magistrate, as well as one of a "conversation held with the mother by an agent of the association." Board-men paraded the great thoroughfares, carrying this appeal:—

PROTESTANT DETECTORAL ASSOCIATION.

NO POPERY!

Abduction of an Infant!
Assault on the Liberty of the Subject!
Mysterious and Awful Proceedings!
Baptism of a Protestant Child in a Convent!

OUTRAGE

Upon the Nation by Foreign Mercenaries!

Every Father and Mother is invited to co-operate in
Maintaining the
PROTESTANT RELIGION,
The Sanctity of Home, and the Inviolability of
BRITISH FREEDOM!

NO SURRENDER!

If there was no coherency in this production, it should
be noted how little that is of the essence of popular appeal. The metropolis was in an uproar. Meetings were
held; subscriptions poured in; . dangerous crowds collected in Winkle Street. When Mr. Dignam Bailey,
Q.C., went down to Westminster to move the Court of
Queen's Bench, multitudes besieged it. Protestant cham-
pions and Papal ecclesiastics vied in their efforts to get
seats. The writ had gone from judge's chambers, re-
turnable to the full court. Sister Suspiciosa, bearing
the infant Ambrosius, and supported by two novices
and Father Certificatus, had been smuggled into court
through mysterious passages in its rear. Mrs. Ginx also,
brought from Rosemary Street by the little man, who
provided her with a bonnet trimmed with orange-colored
ribbons, sat staring with red eyes at her child, now enveloped in a robe that was embroidered with little crosses.

Why need I tell you how dead silence fell upon the
court after the stir caused by the entrance of the judges;
how everybody knew what was coming when a master
beneath the bench rose, and called out, "*Re* Ginx, an
infant, *ex parte* Mary Ginx!" how the chief justice,
fresh and rosy-looking, then blew his nose in a delicate
mauve-colored silk handkerchief; how he tried and discarded half a dozen pens amid breathless silence; how,
in his blandest manner, he said, "Who appears for the
respondent?" and Mr. Dignam Bailey, Q. C., and Mr.
Octavius Ernestus, Q. C., rose together to say that Mr.
Ernestus did?

Mr. Ernestus was a Catholic. He was assisted by
half a dozen counsel. He riddled the affidavits on the
other side, and read voluminous ones on his own; bitterly

animadverted upon the absence of an affidavit by the father; held up to the scorn of a civilized world the course pursued towards his meek and gentle clients by the "fanatical zealots of the Protestant Detectoral Association;" in moving tones referred to the shrinking of "quiet recluses from the gaze of a rude, unsympathizing' world;" cited cases from the time of Magna Charta down; called upon the Court to vindicate Protestant justice; ending his peroration with the aphorism of Lord Mansfield, *Fiat justitia, ruat cœlum!*

One cannot do justice to Mr. Dignam Bailey's argument, when, after lunch, he rose to reply. He was logical and passionate, vindictive and pathetic, by turns. He inveighed against the lady-superior, against her attorneys, against Father Certificatus, against Ginx, — "craven to his heaven-born rights of'political and religious freedom," — against the Roman-Catholic religion, the Pope, the Archbishop of Westminster, the Virgin Mary. The Court knew, and every one else knew, that this was pure pyrotechny; and Mr. Bailey knew that best of all : but though the Bench is swift to speak, slow to hear, it felt obliged, in a case of this public interest, to sit by and be witnesses of the exhibition. Mr. Bailey concluded by a play on the aphorism cited by his learned friend. He would say, that, if such justice were to be done as his friend had urged, the kingdom of heaven in England would rush to its fall."

The Court at once decided, that as the father had confided the custody of the infant to the Sisters of Misery, and did not appear to desire that it should be withdrawn, they, disregarding the religious clouds in which the subject had been too carefully involved on both sides, gave judgment for the defendant, with costs.

As they passed out of court, Mr. Stigma said to his clients, " Quite as I anticipated : you remember I told you so in my opinion."

———◆———

VII.—A PROTESTER, BUT NOT A PROTESTANT.

THE infant Ambrosius and his conductors could scarcely reach the convent in safety. The building showed few windows to the street; but they were all broken. What might have happened in a few days, but that Ginx's Baby took the matter into his own hands, none can say.

The treatment to which the little saint was subjected soured his temper. His kind nurses had choked him twice a day with incense ; and now he had inhaled for seven hours the air of the Queen's Bench. On his return to the convent, he was hastily fed, and carried to the chapel to give thanks for the victory of the day. Wrapped in a handsome chasuble, they laid him on the steps of the altar. In the most solemn part of the service, he coughed and grew sick. The chasuble was bespattered. When the officiating priest, to save that garment, took the child in his arms, he nefariously polluted the sarcerdotal vestments and the altar-steps. Then he kicked toward the altar itself, roared lustily, and finally went into convulsions in Sister Suspiciosa's arms. Like most women, the lady-superior required her enthusiasm to be fed with success. She began to think that she had been cozened : Ginx's Baby was too evidently a spiritual miscarriage. He must, like the rest of his family, be indeed " Protestant to the backbone." Father

Certificatus agreed with her. His robes and best chasuble were befouled.

"Let us not risk a repetition of this conduct," said he. "Let the child be given up. He is baptized, and cannot be severed from the Church. He will return after many days."

Next morning, the solicitors of the Protestant Detectoral Association received a letter from their opponents. In this they said, that, presuming Messrs. Roundhead, Roundhead and Lollard, intended to apply to the Master of the Rolls, the authorities of the convent had decided, after having vindicated themselves in the Queen's Bench, to give up the child, which would be for twenty-four hours at the order and disposal of the association, and afterwards of his parents. "We are instructed by our clients," they added, "to ask you to bear in mind that the child has been admitted and is a member of the Catholic Church, owing allegiance to the Holy Father at Rome, — a bond from which only the Papal excommunication can absolve him."

VIII. — "SEE HOW THESE CHRISTIANS LOVE ONE ANOTHER!"

A MASS-MEETING of Protestants had been summoned for three o'clock on the day designated in the letter of the Papist attorneys, to be held in the Philopragmon Hall. That was the favorite centre of countless movements, both well meant and well executed, and of others as futile as they were foolish. Yet one could not say that a larger proportion of the latter were connected with the hall than existed in as many other human enterprises of any sort. The concession of the Romanists at first dashed the managers of the demonstration. Their grievance was gone. Still there remained topics for a meeting : they would rejoice over victory, and consult about the future of the Protestant baby.

The secretary was an old hand at these meetings. He planned to import into this one a sensation. Ginx's Baby, brought from the convent, stripped of his Papal swathings, and enveloped in a handsome outfit presented by an amiable Protestant duchess, was placed in a cradle, with his head resting on a Bible. I am afraid he was quite as uncomfortable as he had ever been at the convent. When at the conclusion of the chairman's speech, in which he informed the audience of their triumph, this exhibition was deftly introduced upon the platform, the huzzas and clappings, and waving of handkerchiefs, were such as even that place had never seen. The child was astounded into quietness.

Mr. Trumpeter took the chair, believed by many to be, next to the queen, the most powerful defender of the faith in the three kingdoms. I never could understand why the newspapers reported his speeches : I cannot.

When he had done, Lord Evergood, "a popular, practical peer, of sound Protestant principles," as " The Daily Banner " alliteratively termed him next morning, rose to move the first resolution, already cut and dried by the committee : —

" That the infant so happily rescued from the incubus of a delusive superstition should be remitted to the care of the Church Widows' and Orphans' Augmentation Society, and should be supported by voluntary contributions."

Before Lord Evergood could say a word, murmurs

arose in every part of the hall. He was a mild, gentlemanly Christian, without guile; and the opposition both surprised and frightened him. He uttered a few sentences in approval of his proposition, and sat down.

An individual in the gallery shouted, " Sir, I rise to move an amendment! "

Cheers, and cries of " Order, order! — sit down! " &c.

The chairman, with great blandness, said, —

" The gentleman is out of order: the resolution has not yet been seconded. I call upon the Rev. Mr. Valpy to second the resolution."

Mr. Valpy, incumbent of St. Swithin's-Within, insisted on speaking; but what he said was known only to himself. When he had finished, there was an extraordinary commotion. On the platform, many ministers and laymen jumped to their feet; in the hall, at least a hundred aspirants for a hearing raised themselves on benches or the convenient backs of friends.

The chairman shouted, " ORDER, ORDER, gentlemen! This is a great occasion: let us show unanimity! "

There seemed to be a unanimous desire to speak. Amid cheers, cries for order, and Kentish fire, you could hear the Rev. Mark Slowboy, Independent, the Rev. Hugh Quickly, Wesleyan, the Rev. Bereciah Calvin, Presbyterian, the Rev. Ezekiel Cutwater, Baptist, calling to the chair.

A lull ensued, of which advantage was taken by Mr. Stentor, a well-known Hyde-park orator, who bellowed from a friend's shoulders in the pit, " Mr. Chairman, hear *me!* " an appeal that was followed by roars of laughter.

What was the matter? Why, the proposal to hand over the baby to an Anglican refuge stirred up the blood of every Dissenter present. It was lifting the infant out of the frying-pan, and dexterously dropping him into the fire. But the chairman was accustomed to these scenes. He stayed the tumult by proposing that a representative from each denomination should give his opinion to the audience. "Whom would they have first?"

The loudest cries were for Mr. Cutwater, who stood forth, a weak, stooping, half-halting little man, with a limp necktie, and trousers puffy at the knees, but with honest use of them, let me say. It is quite credible, that if Dr. Watts's assertion be true, that

> "Satan trembles when he sees
> The weakest saint upon his knees,"

that arch-enemy was unusually perturbed when Ezekiel Cutwater was upon his. On these he had borne manly contests with evil. Two things, yea, three, were rigid in Ezekiel's creed; fire would never have burned them out of him, — hatred of Popery, contempt of Anglican priestcraft and apostolic succession, and adhesion to the dogma of adult baptism and total immersion. Whoso should not join with him in these, let him be Anathema Maranatha.

His eyes kindled as he looked at the seething audience. "Sir," said he, "I beg to move an amendment to the motion of the noble lord." (Cheers.) "That motion proposes to transfer to the care of the Established Church this tender and unconscious infant (bending over Ginx's Baby) just snatched from the toils of a kindred superstition." (Oh, oh! hisses and cheers.) "I withdraw the expression: I did not mean to be offensive." (Hear.) "This is a grand representative meeting, — not of the English Church, not of the Baptist Church, not of the Wesleyan Church, but of Protestantism." (Cheers and Kentish fire.) "In such an assembly, is it right to propose any singular disposition of a representative infant? This is now the adopted child, not of one, but of all denominations." (Cheers.) "Around his or her — I am not sure which — cherubic head circle the white-winged angels of various churches; and on her or him, whichever it may be," —

The chairman said that he might as well say that he had authentic information that it was *him.*

"Him, then, — concentrate the sympathies of every Protestant heart. Let us not despoil the occasion of its greatness by exhibiting a narrow bigotry in one direction. Let us bring into this infantile focus the rays of Catholic unity." (Loud cheering and Kentish fire.) "To me, for one, it would be eminently painful to think, — what doubtless would occur if the motion is adopted, — that, within a week of his entrance into the asylum of the society named in it, this diminutive and unknowing sinner should go through the farce of a supposititious admission into the Church of Christ." (Oh!) "Yes! I say a farce, whether you regard the age of the acolyte, or the indifferent proportion of water with which it would be performed." (Uproar, oh, oh! and some cheering from the Baptist section.) "But I will not now further enter into these things," said Mr. Cutwater, who knew his cue perfectly well: "I can hold these opinions, and still love my brethren of other denominations. I move, as an amendment, that a committee, consisting of one minister and one layman to be selected from each of the churches, be appointed to take charge of the physical well-being and mental and spiritual training of the infant."

By this proposition, which was received with enthusiasm, Ginx's Baby was to be incontinently pitched into
an arena of polemical warfare. Every one was willing
that a committee should fight out the question vicari-
ously; and therefore, when Mr. Slowboy seconded the
amendment, it was carried with loud acclamations.

But they were not yet out of the wood. On proceed-
ing to nominate members of the committee, the Unitarians and Quakers claimed to be represented. The
platform and the meeting were by the ears again. It
was fiercely contended that only Evangelical Christians
could have a place in such a work; and many of the
nominees declared that they would not sit on a committee with — well, some curious epithets were used.
The Unitarians and Quakers took their stand on the
Catholic principles embodied in the amendment, and on
the fact that Ginx's Baby had now "become national
Protestant property." Mr. Cutwâter and a few others,
moved by the scandal of the dispute, interfered; and the
committee was at length constituted to the satisfaction
of all parties. It was to be called "The Branch Committee of the Protestant Detectoral Union for promoting
the Physical and Spiritual Well-Being of Ginx's Baby."

A fourth resolution was adopted, "That the subject
should be treated in the metropolitan pulpits on the
next sabbath, and a collection taken up in the various
churches for the benefit of the infant." This promised
well for Master Ginx's future.

The meeting had lasted five hours; and, while they
were discussing him, the child grew hungry. In the
tumult, every one had forgotten the subject of it; and,
now it was over, they dispersed without thought of him.

But he would not allow those near him, at all events, to overlook his presence.   Some, foreseeing that awkwardness was impending, slipped away; while three or four staid to ask what was to be done with him.

"Hand him over to the custody of the chairman," said a Mr. Dove.

"I should be most happy," said he smoothly; "but Mrs. Trumpeter is out of town.   Could your dear wife take him, Mr. Dove?"

Mr. Dove's wife was otherwise engaged.

The secretary was unmarried,—chambers at Nincome's Inn.

In the midst of their distress, a woman who had been hanging about the hall, near the platform, came forward, and offered to take charge of him "for the sake of the cause."   Every one was relieved.   After her name and address had been hastily noted, the Protestant baby was placed in her arms.   My Lord Evergood, the chairman, the clergy, the secretary, and the mob went home rejoicing.   Some hours after, Ginx's Baby, stripped of the duchess's beautiful robes, was found by a policeman, lying on a doorstep in one of the narrow streets not a hundred yards behind the Philopragmon.   By an ironical chance, he was wrapped in a copy of the largest daily paper in the world.

IX.—GOOD SAMARITANS, AND GOOD-SAMARITAN TWOPENCES.

AT every breakfast-table in town next morning, the report of the great Protestant meeting was read; and a further report, in leaded type, of the discovery of Ginx's

Baby, at a later period of the evening, by a policeman. A pretty comment on the proceedings! The Good Samaritan put his patient on his ass, and carried him to an inn; while the priest and the Levite, though the latter looked at him, at least let him alone. To have called a public meeting to discuss his fate before deserting him would have been a refinement of inhumanity. The committee were rather ashamed when they met. Instant measures were taken to recover the child, and place him in good hands. The duchess again provided baby-clothes. The next Sunday, sermons were preached on his behalf in a score of chapels. The collections amounted to £800, — a sum increased by donations and subscriptions to the handsome total of £1,360. 10s. 3½d.

It will be seen hereafter what the committee did with the baby; but I happen to have an account of what became of the funds. They were spent as follows, according to a balance-sheet never submitted to the subscribers : —

	£.	s.	d.
Committee-Rooms	45	0	0
Two Secretaries employed by the Committee,	120	0	0
Agents, canvassing, &c.	88	6	2
Printing Notices, Placards, Pamphlets, a "Daily Bulletin of Health," "Life of Ginx's Baby," "Protestant Babyhood, a Tale," "The Cradle of an Infant Martyr," "A Snatched Brand," and other Works issued by the Committee	596	13	5
Advertisements of Meetings, Sermons, &c. .	261	1	1
Legal Expenses	77	6	8
Stationery	35	10	0
Postage, Firing, and Sundries . . .	27	19	2
Total	£1,251	16	6

This left £108. 13s. 9½d. for the baby's keep. No child could have been more thoroughly discussed, preached and written about, advertised, or advised by counsel; but his resources dwindled in proportion to these advantages. Benevolent subscribers too seldom examine the financial items of a report: had any who contributed to this fund seen the balance-sheet, they might have grudged that so little of their bounty went to make flesh, bone, and comfort for the object of it. A cynic would tell them, that to look sharply after the disposal of their guerdon was half the gift. Their indifference was akin to that satirized by the poet, —

" Prodigus et stultus dedit quæ spernit et odit."

In an age of luxury, we are grown so luxurious as to be content to pay agents to do our good deeds for us; but they charge us three hundred per cent for the privilege.

———◆———

X. — THE FORCE; AND A SPECIMEN OF ITS WEAKNESS.

GINX'S BABY had been discovered by a policeman, swaddled in a penny paper distressingly familiar to metropolitan travellers by rail. To omit the details of his treatment at the hands of that great institution, " The Force," would be invidious. The member thereof who fell in with him was walking a back street, sighting doors with his bull's-eye. He was provided with massive boots, so that a thief could hear him coming a hundred yards off; he was personally tall and unwieldy; and a dexterous commissioner had invented a dress designed to enhance these qualities, — a heavy coat, a cart-horse belt, and a round cape. He had been carefully drilled not to walk more than three miles an hour. He was not a little startled when the rays of his lamp fell upon a struggling newspaper, out of which, as from a shell, came mysterious cries. He took up a corner of the paper, and peeped in upon the face of Ginx's Baby; then he occupied a quarter of an hour in embarrassing reflections. A nearly naked child crying in the cold ought to be housed as soon as possible; but X 99 was *on his beat*, and those magic words chained him to certain limits. This, of course, was the rule under a former commissioner; and every one knows that such absurd strategy has been abolished in the existing *régime*. At that time, however, each watchman had his beat, to leave which was neglect of duty, except with a prisoner; and then it was neglect of all the householders within the magic compass. Had X 99 heard the baby crying across the street, which was part of the beat of X 101, he would have passed on with a cheery heart; for the case would have been beyond his jurisdiction. Unhappily, the baby was on his beat; and he was delivered from the temptation of transferring it to the other by the appearance of X 101's bull's-eye not far off. What was he to do? The station was a mile away; the inspector would not arrive for an hour; and it would be awkward, if not undignified, to carry on his rounds a shouting baby wrapped in the largest daily paper. If he left it where it was, and it perished, he might be charged with murder. He was at his wits' end: but, having got there, he resolved on the simplest process; namely, to carry it to the station. No provision was

5

made by the regulations of the force to protect a beat casually deserted even for a proper purpose: hence, while X 99 was absent on his errand of mercy, the valuable shop of Messrs. Trinkett and Blouse, ecclesiastical tailors, was broken into, and several stoles, chasubles, altar-cloths, and other decorative tapestries, were appropriated to profane uses.

At the station, the baby was disposed of according to rule. Due entry was first made in the night-book, by the superintendent, of all the particulars of his discovery. Some cold milk was then procured, and poured down the child's throat. Afterwards, wrapped in a constable's cape, he was placed in a cell, where, when the door was locked, he could not disturb the guardians of the peace.

The same night, in the next cell, an innocent gentleman, seized with an apoplexy in the street, but entered in the charge-sheet as drunk and incapable, died like a dog.

———◆———

XI.—THE UNITY OF THE SPIRIT AND THE BOND OF PEACE.

WHEN the committee met, every one discovered his incongruity with the rest. Each was disposed to treat Ginx's Baby in a different way; in other words, each wished to reflect the views of his particular sect on the object of their charity. They were a new "Evangelical Alliánce," agreed only in hatred to Popery.

Finding at their first meeting that the discussion needed to be brought into a focus, the committee appointed three of their number to draw up a minute of the matters to be argued. This committee reported that there arose respecting the child the following questions : —

"I. — As touching the body : —
  a. Wherewithal he should be fed and clothed ?
  b. In what manner and fashion that should be done ?
II. — As touching the mind and spirit : —
  a. Whether he should be educated ?   If so, —
  b. What were to be the subjects of instruction ?
  c. What creed, if any, should be primarily taught ?
  d. Should he be further baptized ?   If so, —
    1. Into what communion ?
    2. By what ceremonial ? "

This programme, it appeared to its concocters, embraced every thing that concerned Ginx's Baby, except his death by the act of God or the queen's enemies. No sooner was the report made than adopted.   Then a member, eager for the fray, moved the postponement of the first division of questions until the others had been determined.   Why should apostles of truth trouble themselves to serve tables ?   These were very subordinate questions to them; though, I think, of first importance to Ginx's Baby. It was decided to discuss little Ginx's future before considering his present.

The ball was opened by the venerable Archdeacon Hotten, who, amid much excitement, contended, that, from the earliest buddings of thought in an infant mind, religion should be ingrafted upon it, — there could be no education worth the name that was not religious; that with the A should be taught the origin, and with the Z the final destiny and destruction, of evil. To separate education from religion was to clip the wings of the heavenly dove. He asserted that the committee ought at once to have the child baptized in Westminster Abbey, though he was rather of opinion that the previous baptism was canonically valid; that he should be taught the truths of our most holy faith; and, since there could be no faith without a creed, — and the only national creed was that of the Church of England, — the baby should be handed over to the care of a clergyman, and then be sent to a proper religious school. He need not say that he excluded Bugby under its then profane management.

The Church was, however, divided against itself; for the Dean of Triston said he would give more latitude than his very reverend brother. You ought not to define in an infant mind a rigid outline of creed. In fact, he did not acknowledge any creed: he was not obliged to by law, and was disinclined to by his reason. He would rather allow the inner seeds of natural light — the glorious, all-pervading efflorescence of the Deity in all men's hearts — to grow within the young spirit. The dean was assuredly vague, and far less earnest than his brother cleric.

The "Rev." Mr. Bumpus, Unitarian, met the suggestions of the archdeacon with the scorn they merited. It was impossible to apply to a representative child of an enlightened age theories so long exploded. The dean had certainly come nearer the truth with that broad sympathy for which he was noted. He himself proposed that the child should be made a model nursling of the liberalism of a new era. Old things were passing away : all things had become new. Creeds were the discarded banners of a mediæval past, fit only to be hung up in the churches, and looked at as historic monuments; nevermore to be flaunted in the front of battle! The education of the day was that which taught a man the introspection whereby he recognized the divine within himself, — under any aspect, under any tuition, whether of Brahma, Confucius, or Christ. Truth was kaleidoscopic, and varied with the media through which it was viewed. As for the child, every aspect of truth and error should be allowed to play upon his mind. Let him acquire ordinary school learning for fifteen years, and then send him to the London University.

Here the chairman, and half a dozen members of the committee, protested that the said university was a school of the Devil; and several interchanges of discourtesy took place.

Mr. Shortt, M.P., begged to suggest, as a matter of business, that, for the present, the child was not capable of receiving any ideas whatever, and might die, or prove to be dumb or an idiot, and so require no education. Ought they not to postpone this discussion until the subject was old enough to be worth consideration?

It was Mr. Shortt's habit to show his practical vein by business-like obstructions of this kind. He had been able a score of times to demonstrate to the House of Commons how silly it was to consider probabilities. In fact, he was opposed heart and soul to prophetic legislation : he would live, legislatively, from hand to mouth.

But the committee would not allow Mr. Shortt to run away with the bone of contention.

The Rev. Dr. M'Gregor Lucas, of the National Cale-
donian Believers, had been silent too long to contain
himself further. This man needs some particular de-
scription whenever his name is made public. Nay, for
this he lives; and by it, some think. At all events, he
appears to be equally eager for rebuke and applause :
they both involve notoriety, and notoriety is sure to pay.
Few absurdities had been overlooked by his shallow ingenuity. Simply to have invested his limited mental
endowments in trying to make the world believe him a
genius would have been only so like what many thousands are doing as to have absolved him from too harsh
a judgment; but he traded in perilous stuff. Cheap
prophecy was his staple. It was his wont to give out
about once in five years that the world would shortly
come to an end; and, like Mr. Zadkiel, he found people who thought their inevitable disappointment a
proof of his inspiration. Had you heard the honeyed
words dropping from his lips, you would have taken him
for a Scotch angel, and, consequently, a rarity. Could
such lips utter harsh sayings, or distil vanities? Show
him a priest, and you would hear! The pope was his
particular born foe; popery his enemies' country: so
he said. It was safe for him to stand and throw his
darts. No one could say whether they hit, or did not;
while most spectators had the good will to hope that
they did. How he would have lived if Daniel and St.
John had dreamed no dreams, one cannot conjecture :
as it was, they provided the doctor with endless open-
ings for his fancy. Since no one could solve the riddle
of their prophecies, it was certain that no one could
disprove his solutions. Yet these came so often to their

own disproof by lapse of time, that I can only think that
the good doctor hoped to die before his critical periods
came, or was so clever as to trust the infallibility of human weakness.

I describe Dr. Lucas at so great a length, because it
will be easier and more-edifying to the reader to conceive what he said than for me to recount it. He
showed the baby to be one of seven mysteries. He was
in favor of teaching him at once to hate idolatry, music,
crosses, masses, nuns, priests, bishops, and cardinals.
The "humanities," the Shorter Catechism, the Confes-
sion of Faith, and "The Whole Duty of Man," would, in
his opinion, be the books to lay the groundwork in the
child's mind of a Christian character of the highest
type.

Mr. Ogle, M.P., here vigorously intervened. Said
he, —

"I can't, with all deference, agree to any of these
suggestions. They involve hand-to-hand fighting over
this baby's body. No one of us is entitled to take
charge of him: else why did we all unite to rescue
him from the nunnery? He will be torn to pieces
among contending divines! I think a purely secular
education is all that, as a committee, we should aim at.
We have but just withdrawn the child from the shadow
of a single ecclesiastical influence: would you transfer
it to another? Every Protestant denomination is con-
tributing to his support: how can you devote their gifts
to rearing him for one? You would have no peace:
better at once treat him as the man of Benjamin treated
his wife, — cut him up into enough pieces to send to all
the tribes of Israel, summoning them to the fight. I say,

we have nothing to do with this just now: let him be
educated in a secular academy, and let each sect be free
to send its agents to instruct him out of school-hours as
they please."

The Rev. Theodoret Verity, M.A., rose in anger.

"Surely, sir, you cannot seriously propound such a
scheme! Would you leave this precious waif to be buf-
feted between the contending waves of truth and error,
in the vague hope, that, by some lucky wind, he might
finally be cast upon a rock of safety? I protest against
all these educational heresies: they are redolent of brim-
stone. Truth is truth, or there is none at all. If there
be any, it is our duty to impart it to this immortal at the
outset of his existence. Secular education!—what do
you mean by it? Who shall sever one question from
another, and call one secular, and the other religious?
Is not every relation and every truth in some way or
other connected with religion?" &c. Mr. Verity has
been saying the same thing any time these forty years.

"Forgive me," replied Mr. Ogle, "if I say that this is
very vague talking. I have not proposed to sever one
question from another. I only propose to do in a different way that which is being done now by the most
rigid of Mr. Verity's friends. It is impossible to com-
prehend what is meant by such a statement as that
every truth is somehow connected with religion. It may
be that the notion—if it really is not, as I suspect it to
be, mere verbiage and clap-trap, used by certain fools to
mislead others—means that there is some such coherency between all truths as there is, for instance, between
the elements of the body. I would admit that; but is
not blood a different and perfectly severable thing from

bone? Each has its place, office, relation. But who would say that one could not be regarded by a physicist in the largest variety of its aspects apart from the other? Yet the physicist comes back again to consider with respect to each its relations to all the rest: the separate study has rather prepared him for more profound insight into those relations. Thus it is with the body of truth. In spite of Mr. Verity, I affirm that there are truths that have not in themselves any element of religion whatever. The forty-seventh proposition of Euclid will be taught by a Jesuit precisely as it is taught in the London University. Geography will affirm certain principles, and designate places, rivers, mountains, that no faith can remove and cast into unknown seas. These subjects and others are taught in our most bigoted schools, in separate hours and relations from religion. What, then, do you mean by affirming that there can be no secular education of this child apart from religious teaching? We are not likely to agree, if I may judge from what I have seen, on any one method of religious instruction for it: therefore I wish first to fix common bounds within which our common benevolence may work. Well, we all go to the Bible. We agree that between its covers lies religious truth somewhere. If you like, let him have that; and let him have some kindly and holy influences about him in the way of practice and example, such as many of our sects can supply many instances of. Give him no catechism: let him read a creed in our daily life. The articles of faith strongest in his soul will be those which have crystallized there from the combined action of truth and experience, and not, as it were, been pasted on its walls by ecclesiastical bill-posters. 'What is truth?'

he must ask and answer for himself, as we all must do before God. Don't mistake me: I hope I am not more indifferent to religion than any here present; but I differ from them on the best method of imbuing the mind and heart with it. Surely we need not, we cannot, — it would be an exquisite absurdity, — pass a resolution in this committee that the child is to be a Calvinist! Who, then, would agree to secure him from any taint of Arminian heresy in years to come? Dare you even resolve that he shall be a Christian and a Protestant? I would not insure the risk. But, with so many of Christ's followers about me, surely, surely, without providing any ecclesiastical mechanism, there will be testified to him simply how he may be saved. Your prayers, your visits, your kindly moral influence and talk, your living example of a goodness derived not from dogmas, but from affectionate following of a holy pattern, and trust in revealed mercies, your pointing to that pattern, and showing the daily passage of these mercies, will prompt his search after the truth that has made you what you are. Let some good woman do for him a mother's part; but choose her for her general goodness, and not for the dogmas of her church. The simpler her piety, the better for him, I should say!'"

This straightforward speech fell like a new apple of discord in the midst of the committee. Angry knots were formed, and the noble chairman found that he could not restore order. An adjournment was agreed to. Luckily for the body of Ginx's Baby, he had been meanwhile sent to a home where Protestant money secured to him, for the time, good living, while his benefactors were discussing what to do with his soul.

Surely it were no impertinence to interrupt this history, and advert to the fact, that, in the discussion just related, every one was, to some extent, right, and to some extent agreed. That religious teaching was due to an immortal spirit, — some notion and evidence of the Divine and the great hereafter to be conveyed to it, — scarce was disputed. Nor was there collison over the necessity of what is called intellectual cultivation. The boy must be taught something of the world in which he was to live; nay, this latter knowledge seemed to be most immediately practical. As each disputant fixed his eye on one or the other aim, that end appeared to him to be the most important. · Hence, by a natural lapse, they came to treat subjects as antagonistic which were, in fact, parallel and quite consistent. The one called the others godless : the others threw back the aspersion of bigotry. Then came complication. What was "religion " ? Intellectual culture they could agree about, — it embraced well-known areas, — but this religion divided itself into many disputable fields. These brother Protestants were like country neighbors, who must encounter each other at fairs, markets, meets, and balls, and smile and greet, though each at heart is looking savagely at the other's landmarks, and most are, very likely, fighting bitter lawsuits all the while. It was because religion meant CREED to most members of the committee, and because it so implies to the vast bodies they represented, that they could not come to terms about Ginx's Baby or any other infantile immortal. Not always, perhaps, but often, they fought for futile distinctions. Had Mahomet's creed consisted of but one article, "*There is one God*," the blood of many nations might never have given testimony against the creed they resented when to it he tacked, "*and Mahomet is his prophet.*" Could Protestants but consent to agree in their agreement, and peacefully differ in their petty differences, how would the aggregated impulse of a simple faith roll down before it all the impediments of error!

When Ginx's Baby had grown to a discretionary age, and was at all able to know truth from error (supposing that to be knowable), there were in the country fifty thousand reverend gentlemen of every tincture of religious opinion who might ply him with their various theories; yet few of these would be contented unless they could seize him while his young nature was plastic, and try to imprint on immortal clay the trade-mark of some human invention.

———◆———

XII.—No Funds, no Faith, no Works.

THE Committee of the Protestant Detectoral Union on Ginx's Baby held twenty-three meetings. They were then as far from unity of purpose as when they set out. Variety was given to the meetings by the changing combinations of members in attendance. The finances were little heeded in the intensity of their zeal for truth. These at length fell altogether into the hands of the association's secretary, and, we have seen, involved large items of expense. The twenty-three meetings extended over a year. At the end of that time, the secretary startled the committee by laying on the table a demand for the board and keep of the Protestant baby for three months, amounting to £36; and adding, that the sum in

hand was £1. 4s. 4½d. In his report he said, " No effort
has been spared, by means of advertisements, pamphlets,
tales, leaders and paragraphs in newspapers and religious journals, together with occasional sermons, to
maintain the public interest in this child ; but attention
has been diverted from him by the great Roman Spozzi
case, and the anxiety created throughout the Protestant
world by the recent discovery, made by Dr. Gooddee, of
a solitary survivor of the ancient Church of the Vieux-
bois Protestants in a secluded valley of the Pyrenees."

The secretary asked the committee to provide the
money to discharge the baby's liabilities ; but they instantly adjourned, and no effort could afterwards get a
quorum together. When the persons who had charge
of the Protestant foundling discovered the state of
affairs, they began to dun the secretary, and to neglect
the child, now about thirteen months old and preparing
to walk. Since no money appeared, they sold whatever
clothes had been provided for him, and absconded from
the place where they had been farming him for Protestantism. The secretary, by chance hearing of this, was
discreet enough to make no inquiries. Ginx's Baby,
" as a Protestant question," vanished from the world. I
never heard that any one was asked what had been done
with the funds ; but I have already furnished the account that ought to have been rendered.

XIII. — In Transitu.

ONE night, near twelve o'clock, a shrewd tradesman,
looking out of his shop-door before he turned into bed,

heard a cry, which proceeded from a bundle on the
pavement.   This he discovered to be an infant wrapped
in a potato-sack.   He was quick enough to observe that
it had been deftly laid over a line chiselled across the
pavement to the corner of his house; which line he
knew to be the boundary between his own parish of St.
Simon Magus and the adjacent parish of St. Bartimeus.
He took note, being a business-man, of the exact position of the child's body in relation to this line, and then
conveyed it to the workhouse of the other parish.

PART III.

WHAT THE PARISH DID WITH HIM.

I.—PAROCHIAL KNOTS; TO BE UNTIED WITHOUT PREJUDICE.

THE infant borne to the workhouse of St. Bartimeus was Ginx's Baby. When he had been placed on the floor of the matron's room, and examined by the master, that official turned to the unwelcome bearer of the burden : —

" Did you find this child?"

" Yes."

" Where ? "

" Lying opposite my shop, in Nether Place."

" What's your name ? "

" Doll."

" Oh! you're the cheesemonger. Your shop's on the other side of the boundary, in the other parish. The child ought not to come here : it doesn't belong to us."

" Yes, it does : it wasn't on my side of the line."

" But it was in front of your house ? "

" Well, the line runs crosswise : it don't follow the child was in our parish."

" Oh, nonsense! there's no doubt about it! We can't take the child in. You must carry it away again."

79

Mr. Snigger turned to leave the room.

"Wait a bit, sir," said Mr. Doll. "I shall leave the child here, and you can do as you like with it. It ain't mine, at all events. I say, it lay in your parish ; and, if you don't look after it, you may be the worse of it. The coroner's sure to try to earn his fees. Good-night!"

He hurried from the room.

"Stop!" shouted the master, "I say: I don't accept the child. You leave it here at your own risk. We keep it without prejudice, remember; without prejudice, sir!— without" —

Mr. Doll was in the street, and out of hearing.

II. — A Board of Guardians.

THE guardians of St. Bartimeus met the day after Mr. Doll's clever stratagem. Among other business was a report from the master of the workhouse, that a child, name unknown, found by Mr. Doll, cheesemonger, of Nether Place, in the Parish of St. Simon Magus, opposite his shop, and, as he alleged, on the nearer side of the parish boundary, had been left at the workhouse, and was now in the custody of the matron. The guardians were not accustomed to restrain themselves, and did not withhold the expression of their indignation upon this announcement. As Mr. Doll had himself been a guardian of St. Simon Magus, it was clear to their impartial minds that he was trying by a trick to foist a bastard — perhaps his own — on the wrong parish.

Mr. Cheekey, a licensed victualler, moved that the master's report be put under the table.

Mr. Slinkum, draper, seconded the motion.

Mr. Edge, ironmonger, pointed out that there was no parliamentary precedent for such a disposition of the report; and, further, that such action did not dispose of the baby.

" Well," said Mr. Cheekey, turning painfully red, " no matter how ye put it. I move to get rid of the brat. What's the best form of motion ? "

A churchwarden, who happened to be a gentleman, explained that the board could not dismiss the question in so summary a way. " He could foresee that there might be a nice point of law in the case. They would have to take some legal means of ascertaining their liabilities, and of forcing the other parish to take the child if they ought to do so. They must consult their solicitor."

This gentleman was sent for post-haste. Meanwhile, the baby was ordered to be brought in for inspection. The matron had handed him over to a sort of half-witted inmate of the house, whose wits, however, were strangely about him at the wrong time, to nurse and amuse him. This person brought Ginx's Baby into the board-room, and placed him on the table. The board of guardians took a good look at him. He was not then in fair condition. He was limp, he was dirty, hollow in the cheeks, white, stiff in his limbs, and half naked (to be regardless of gender), —

" Pallidula, rigida, nud·ula."

" Hum l " said Mr. Stink, who was a dog-breeder, " what's his pedigree ? "

6

This brutal joke was well received by some of the guardians.

"His pedigree," answered the half-wit gravely, "goes back for three hundred years. Parients unknown by name, but got by Misery out o' Starvashun. The line began with Poverty out o' Laziness in Queen Elizabeth's time. The breed has been a large 'un, wotever you thinks of the quality."

This pleasantry was less acceptable to the board.

"Well," said Mr. Scoop, grocer, a great stickler for parliamentary modes of procedure, "I move it be committed."

"Committed! Where?" said Mr. Stink.

"To Newgate, I s'pose," said the half-wit, his eyes twinkling.

"Nonsense, sir! — for consideration. Send that man out!" exclaimed Scoop: "clear the room for consultation!"

Davus was expelled, and the baby was then formally consigned to the care of a committee. By this time, the legal adviser came in. The facts having been stated to him, he said, —

"Gentlemen, as at present advised, I am of opinion that the parish in which the child was found is bound to maintain him. If Mr. Doll (a highly respectable person, my own cheesemonger) found the child beyond the boundaries of St. Simon Magus, — and he will, of course, swear that he did, — you cannot refuse to take it in. However, I had better ascertain the facts from Mr. Doll, and take the opinion of counsel. Meanwhile, we must beware not to compromise ourselves by admitting any thing, or doing any thing equivalent to an admission.

Let me see, — ah! — yes, — a notice to be served on the
other parish, repudiating the infant; another notice to
Mr. Doll to take it away, and that it remains here at his
risk and expense. You see, gentlemen, we could hardly
venture to return it to Mr. Doll: we should create an
unhappy impression in the minds of the public " —

" D——n the public! " said Mr. Stink.

" Quite so, my dear sir," said Mr. Phillpotts, smiling,
—" quite so; but that is not a legal, or, in fact, practicable
mode of discarding them : we must act with public opinion, I fear. Then, to resume, thirdly, and to be strictly
safe, we must serve a notice on the infant and all whom
it may concern. I think I'll draft it at once."

In a few minutes, the committee in charge pinned to
the only garment of Ginx's Baby a paper in the following form : —

PARISH OF ST. BARTIMEUS.

To —— —— *(name unknown), a Foundling, and all other
persons interested in the said Foundling.*

TAKE NOTICE,

*That you, or either of you, have no just or lawful claim to have
you or the said infant chargeable on the said parish. And this
is to notify, that you, the said infant, are retained in the workhouse of the said parish under protest ; and that whatsoever is
or may be done or provided for you is at the proper charge of
you, and all such persons as are and were by law bound to maintain and keep the same.*

WINKLE & PHILLPOTTS,
Solicitors for the Board.

WHEN Mr. Phillpotts called upon Doll, the cheese-monger, the latter straightway gave him the facts as they had occurred. He pointed out the exact spot on which the bundle had lain; he gave an estimate of the number of inches on each side of the line occupied by it, and declared that the head and shoulders of the infant lay in the parish of the solicitor's clients. Ginx's Baby, under the title "*Re* a Foundling," was once more submitted for the opinion of counsel. They advised the board, that as the child was in both parishes when found, but had been taken up by a rate-payer of St. Simon Magus, the latter parish was bound to support him. Whereupon the guardians of St. Bartimeus at their next meeting resolved that the vestry of the other parish should have a written notice to remove the child; failing which, application should be made to the Queen's Bench for a *mandamus* to compel them to do it.

On receiving the challenge, the guardians of St. Simon Magus also took counsel's opinion. They were advised, that as the greater part, and especially the head, of the infant, was, when discovered, in the parish of St. Bartimeus, the latter was clearly chargeable. Both parties then proceeded to swear affidavits. The attorney-general and solicitor-general, the two great law-officers of the crown, were retained on opposite sides, and took fees, — not for an imperial prosecution, but as petty queen's counsel in an inter-parochial squabble.

IV. — WITHOUT PREJUDICE TO ANY ONE BUT THE GUARDIANS.

THE Court of Queen's Bench, after hearing an elaborate statement from the attorney-general, granted a rule *nisi* for a *mandamus*. This rule was entered for argument in a paper called "The Special Paper;" and, the list being a heavy one, nearly a year elapsed before it was reached. It was then again postponed several times "for the convenience of counsel."

The Board of St. Bartimeus chafed under the law's delay. They became morbidly sensitive to the incubus of Ginx's Baby, especially as the press had been reviewing some of their recent acts with great bitterness. The guardians were defiant. Having served their notices, they were induced by Mr. Stink to resolve not to maintain the infant. The poor child was threatened with dissolution. Thus, no doubt, many difficulties in parochial administration are solved, — the subject vanishes away. The baby was kept provisionally in a room at the workhouse. On the outside of the door was a notice in fair round-hand : —

NOTICE.

DOLL'S FOUNDLING.

Pending the legal inquiry into the facts concerning the above infant, and a decision as to its settlement, all officials, assistants, and servants of the workhouse are forbidden to enter the room in which it is deposited, or to render it any service or assistance, on pain of dismissal. No food is to be supplied to it from the workhouse kitchen.

N. B. — This is not intended to prevent persons other than officials, &c., from having access to the infant, or assisting it.

BY ORDER OF THE BOARD.

That any body of human beings other than Patago-
nians could have coolly contemplated such a result as
must have followed upon the strict performance of this
order would be incredible except in the instance of the
guardians of St. Bartimeus.   There was nothing they
could not do, or leave undone.   Fortunately for Ginx's
Baby, the order was disobeyed.   Occasionally, lady-
visitors went to look at him and give him some food.
He was toddling about the room on unsteady legs; but
Charity seemed to be appalled by the official questions
hanging about this child.   The master, Snigger, whose
business it was every day to ascertain whether the cause
of the great parochial quarrel was in or out of existence,
became a traitor to the board.   When the child grew.
hungry and dangerously thin, he brought bottles of pap
prepared by Mrs. Snigger, and administered it to him.
No conclusions to the disfavor of the board were to be
drawn from this conduct; for Snigger was particular to
say to the boy in a loud voice, each time he fed him, —

"Now, youngster, this is without prejudice : remember !
I give you due notice, — without prejudice."

Who, in Master Ginx's situation, would have had any
prejudices to such action, or have expressed them, even
if they were entertained ?   He took no objection as he
took the pap; while Snigger was glad to be able to do
an unusual kindness without compromising the parish.

Thus things had gone on for many months, when one
day an eye of that Argus monster, the public, was set
upon Ginx's Baby.   A well-known nobleman, calling at
the workhouse to see a little girl whom he had saved
from infamy, as he passed down a corridor was arrested
by the notice on the door of our hero's room.   Curiosity

took him in, and horror chained him there for some time. Had he not entered, Ginx's Baby, spite of Snigger, would in twenty-four hours have ceased to supply facts to history. He was suffering from low fever; and his condition was as sensationally shocking as any reporter could have wished. Out rushed the peer for a doctor; took a cab to a magistrate, and detailed the whole case, to be repeated in next morning's papers. Penny-a-liners ran to the spot, wrote vivid descriptions of the baby and the room, and transcribed the notice. The guardians were drubbed in trenchant leaders and indignant letters. They, instead of bending to the storm, strove to confront it, and passed angry resolutions of a childish and grotesque character. The few of them who possessed any sense of propriety were railed at in the meetings till they ceased to attend. The uproar outside increased. Why did not the president of the poor-law board interfere? At last he did interfere; that is, instead of visiting the scene himself, and satisfying his own eyes as to the truth of what his ears had heard, — a process that would have taken a couple of hours, — he appointed a gentleman to hold an inquiry. The guardians became furious. The reports of their proceedings read like the vagaries of a lunatic-asylum or the deliberations of the American Senate. They discharged Snigger for breach of orders, substituting a relative of Mr. Stink. They put a lock on the door, and passed food to the baby by a stick. A committee was appointed to see him fed; and they forwarded a memorial to the poor-law board, stating that "he daily had more food than he could possibly eat, and was in admirable condition." They refused to allow any doctor but one employed by themselves to see him.　They procured from him a certificate that the noble busybody and his physician had made a mistake, and that all the functions of life in the infant appeared to be in perfect order. Then came the gentleman and the inquiry, and his report, and a letter from the poor-law board, and further discussions and more letters, until the bewildered public gnashed its teeth at the minister, the guardians, and the law, and wished them all at Land's End, or beyond it.

---◆---

V. — An Ungodly Jungle.

The case of the Guardians of St. Bartimeus against the Guardians of St. Simon Magus was at length reached. The argument lasted for two days.　There is a grim work, the short title whereof is " Burns's Justice," in five fat volumes, from which the legal Dryasdust turns aghast.　In one of these portentous books, title " Poor," pp. 1200, the inquisitive may find a code unrivalled by the most malignant ingenuity of former or contemporary nations, — a code wherein, by gradual accretion, has been framed a system of relief to poverty and distress so impolitic, so unprincipled, that none but the dryest, mustiest, most petrified parish-official could be expected to lift up his voice to defend it; so complicated, that no man under heaven knows its length or breadth or height or depth : yet it stands to this hour a monument of English stolidity, a marvel of lazy or ignorant statesmanship.　Imagine, if you please, a lord chief justice and three puisnes, all keen, practical men, alive to public policy and the common-weal, eager to extricate the truth and do the right, plunging into this "ungodly jungle," thwarted at every turn in search of justice for Ginx's Baby. With all his patient industry and lightning quickness of apprehension, the chief justice found it hard to reconcile past and present, or evolve from the vast confusion any thing consistent with his moral instincts.

Clear the board, gentlemen! True regenerative legislation will begin by drawing away the rubbish. Reform means more than repair. Mend, patch; take down a little here, prop up some tottering nuisance there; fill in gaping chinks with patent legislative cement; coat old façades with bright paint; hide decay beneath a gloze of novelty; titivate, decorate, furbish, — and, after all, your house is not a new one, but a whited sepulchre shaking to decay. Repair? There is a Repair party, intermediating between Tories and Reformers, — Radicals or Rooters let us call these latter, if you like, — who cling to "vested interests" and all other sorts of antique nuisances, yet say they are willing to improve them. REFORM, which means, pull down with bold statesman's hand, and with like hand REBUILD, is no darling of your political repairer. Call the party and the men by their right names; and give me, for utility in legislation or administrative action, an old Tory and obstructive party, rather than this middling, meddling, muddling repairer, —

"Eager to change, yet fearful to destroy."

Just now, all social reformation, in its noblest aims and attempts, is fettered by the Repair party. What is termed sanitary reform is enfeebled, and the vigor withdrawn from it, by this party. "Vested rights," "the liberty of the people," "interference with personal freedom," "EXPENSE," — these are the watchwords of the Repairer, in opposition to him, who, pointing to the pallor and fever of a hundred neighborhoods, calls upon a ministry to cleanse them with imperial force.

A comprehensive scheme of national education is seized and half throttled by the Repair party. "Oh! utilize what there is; improve on and tack to the denominational system; avail yourself of the jealousy of sects; see what a grand building that has already erected! True, it is not large enough; true, it is badly built: but repair that, and add wings. It will cost you ever so much to rebuild. Repair!"

The methods of relief to the poor are old, cumbrous, unequal, — as stupid as those who administer them. Forth steps the reformer, and cries out, "Clear this wrack away! Get rid of your antiquated Bumbledom, your parochial and non-parochial distinctions, your complicated map of local authorities; re-distribute the kingdom on some more practical system, redress the injustice of unequal rating, improve the machinery and spirit of relief, and so on." You have the Repair party shouting its *Non possumus* as loudly as any other arch-obstructive: "Heaven forbid! Queen Elizabeth and the poor-laws forever! To the rescue of local government and vested interests! Repair!"

Some one with a long head and a divinely-warmed heart, searching vainly for help to thousands in the packed alleys of his English home, sends his quick glance across seas to rich lands that daily cry to heaven for strong arms that wield the plough and spade. "Ho!" he shouts, "labor to land; starvation to production; death unto life!" And he calls upon every statesman and patriot to help the good work, and give their energies to frame an emigration scheme. Then the Repair party foams: "Send away the labor, the source of our wealth? No! Mend the condition of the laborer; give him the sop of political rights, — free breakfasts, the ballot. Give State funds to alter social conditions? No! Improve the methods of local assistance to emigration : it is a temporary remedy. Repair!"

Thus, according to the gospel of this party, every thing must be subject of restoration only. Like antiquarians, they utter groans over the abolition of any thing, however ugly it may be, however unfitted for human uses, and with however so elegant a piece of artistry you desire to displace it. For them a Gilbert Scott politician, reverential restorer of bygone styles, enthusiastic to conserve and amend the grotesque Gothic policies of the past, rather than some Brunel or Stephenson statesman, engineering in novel mastery of circumstances, — not fearful to face and conquer even the antique impediments of Nature. Give me a trenchant statesman, or, I pray you, leave legislation alone. Better things as they are than patched to distraction.

At length, by means of some delicate legal adjustments, the judges saw their way to affirming that Ginx's Baby's parish was that of St. Bartimeus, and refused the rule for a *mandamus*.

VI.—PAROCHIAL BENEVOLENCE; AND ANOTHER TRANSLATION.

THE authorities of St. Bartimeus did not take kindly to
the charge imposed upon them by the Queen's Bench.
Some of the guardians privately hinted to the master
that it was unnecessary to overfeed the infant. They
did not burthen him with much clothing; and what he
had was shared with many lively companions. When
you, good matron, look at your little pink-cheeked daugh-
ter, so clean and so cosey in her pretty cot, waking to see
the well-faced nurse, or you, still sweeter to her eyes,
watching above her dreams, perhaps you ought to stop
a moment to contrast the scene with the sad tableaux
you may get sight of not far away. . . . Ginx's Baby
was not an ill-favored child. He had inherited his father's frame and strength : these helped him through the
changes we are relating. What if these capacities had,
by simple nourishing food, cleanly care-taking, and
brighter, kindlier associations, been trained into full
working order ? Left alone or ill tended, they were daily
dwindling; and the depreciation was going on not solely
at the expense of little Ginx, but of the whole community. To reduce his strength one-half was to reduce
one-half his chances of independence, and to multiply
the prospects of his continuous application for STATE
AID.

The money spent in stopping a hole in a Dutch dike
is doubtless better invested than if it were to be retained until a vast breach had laid half a kingdom under
water. Surely your Hollander would agree to be
mulcted in one-third of his fortune rather than run the
hazard.

Every day through this wealthy country there are men and women busy marring the little images of God that are by and by to be part of its public, shadowing young spirits, repressing their energy, sapping their vigor or failing to make it up, corrupting their nature by foul associations moral and physical. Some are doing it by special license of the Devil, others by act of Parliament, others by negligence or niggardliness. Could you teach or force these people — many unconsciously engaged in the vile work — to run together, as men alarmed by sudden danger, and throw around a helpless generation influences and a care more akin to your own home-ideal, would you not transfigure the next epoch? would not your labor and sacrifice be a GOD-WORK, reaching out weighty, fruit-laden branches far into the grateful future? 'Tis by feeling and enjoining everywhere the need of such a movement as this that you, O all-powerful woman! can carry your will into the play of a great economic and social reform. Society that recognizes not a root-truth like that is sowing the wind: God knows what it will reap.

So the guardians, keeping carefully within the law, neglected nothing that could sap little Ginx's vitality, deaden his happiest instincts, derange moral action, cause hope to die within his infant breast almost as soon as it were born. Good God!

The items the board were really entitled to charge the rate-payers as supplied to our hero were —

Dirt,

Fleas,

Foul air,

Chances of catching skin-diseases, fevers, &c.,

Vile company,

Neglect,

Occasional cruelty, and

A small supply of bad food and clothing.

Every pauper was to them an obnoxious charge, by any
and every means to be reduced to a *minimum* or *nil.*
Ginx's Baby was reduced to a *minimum.* His constitution enabled him to protest against reduction to *nil.*
But just after the bills of costs had been taxed, mulct-
ing the rate-payers of St. Bartimeus in a sum of more
than £1,600, the guardians were made aware of the
name and origin of their charge. One of the persons
who had deserted him was arrested for theft; and among
other articles in her possession were some of the baby's
clothes. She confessed the whole story, and declared
that the child left in Nether Place was no other than
the Protestant Baby, son of Ginx, about whom so much
stir had been made two years before. The guardians
were not long in tracing Ginx; and at his quarters in
Rosemary Street the hapless changeling was one day
delivered by a deputy relieving-officer, with the benedic-
tion, by me sadly recorded, —

" There he is, d—n him ! "

I am sure, if the guardians had been there, they would
have said, —

" Amen ! "

PART IV.

WHAT THE CLUBS AND POLITICIANS DID WITH HIM.

I.—MOVED ON.

GINX'S BABY'S brothers and sisters would have nothing to say to him; Mrs. Ginx declared she could see in him no likeness to her own dear lost one; and her husband swore that the brat never was his. The couple had latterly been pinching themselves and their children to save enough to emigrate. For this purpose, aid and counsel were given to them by a neighboring curate, whose name, were my pages destined to immortality, should be printed here in golden letters. Rich and full will be his sheaves when many a statesman reaps tares. Finding that a thirteenth child was imposed on them by so superior a force as the law of England, the Ginxes hastened their departure.

Their last night in London, towards the small hours, Ginx, carrying our hero, went along Birdcage Walk. He scarcely knew where he was going, or how he was about to dispose of his burden; but he meant to get rid of it. On he went, here and there met by shadowy creatures, who came towards his footsteps in the uncer-

95

tain darkness, and, when they could see that he was no quarry for them, flitted away again into the night.

He passed the dingy houses (since replaced by the Foreign Office), across the open space before the Horse Guards, near the house of a popular prime-minister, and up the broad steps, till he stood under the York Column.

The shadow of this was an inviting place; but a policeman, turning his lantern suspiciously on the man walking about at that silent hour with a child in his arms, frustrated his wish. Slowly Ginx tramped along Pall Mall, with only one other creature stirring, as it seemed for the moment, — a gentleman who turned up the steps of a large building. Seating the child on the bottom step, and telling him not to cry, Ginx instantly crossed the road, turned into St. James's Square, passed by the rails, and, stealing from corner to corner through the mazes of that locality, reached home by way of Piccadilly and Grosvenor Place. Henceforth this history shall know him no more.

II. — CLUB IDEAS.

SCARCELY had the shadow of his parent vanished in the gloom before Ginx's Baby piped forth a lusty protest: the street rang again. Ere long, the doors at the top of the steps swung back, and a portly form stood in the light.

" Halloo! what's the matter? " (This was a general observation into space.) " Why, bless my heart! here's a child crying on the steps! "

Another form appeared.

"Is there nobody with it ? Halloo! any one there ? "

No answer came save from poor little Ginx; but his was decided. The two servants descended the steps, and looked at the miserable boy without touching him. Then they peered into the darkness, in hope that they might get a glimpse of his mother or a policeman. A rapid step sounded on the pavement, and a gentleman came up to the group.

" What have we here ? " he said gently.

" It's a child, Sir Charles, I found crying on the steps. I expect it's a trick to get rid of him. We are looking for a policeman to take him away."

"Poor little fellow!" said Sir Charles, stooping to take a fair look at Ginx's Baby; "for you and such as you the policeman or the parish-officers are the national guardians, and the prison or the poor-house the home. . . . Bring him into the club, Smirke."

The men hesitated a moment before executing so unwonted a demand; but Sir Charles Sterling was a man not safely to be thwarted, — a late minister, and a member of the committee. The child, being carried into the magnificent hall of the club, stood on its mosaic floor. From above, the radiance of the gas " sunlight " streamed down over the marble pillars, and glanced on gilded cornices and panels of scagliola. A statue of the Queen looked upon him from the niche that opened to the dining-room; another of the great Puritan soldier, statesman, and ruler, with his stern, massive front ; and yet another, with the strong yet gentle features of the champion free-trader, seemed to regard him from their several corners. On the walls around were portraits of men who had striven for the deliverance of the people

7

from ancient yokes and fetters. Of course, Ginx's Baby did not see all this. He, poor boy! dazed, stood with a knuckle in his eye, while the porter, lackeys, Sir Charles Sterling, and others who strolled out of the reading-room, curiously regarded him. But any one observing the scene apart might have contrasted the place with the child, — the principles and the professions whereof this grandeur was the monument and consecrated taber-nacle with this solitary atomic specimen of the material whereon they were to work. What social utility had re-sulted from the great movements initiated by them who erected and frequented this place? Ought they to have had, and did they still need, a complement? While wonderful political changes had been wrought, and bene-fits not to be exaggerated won for many classes, WHAT HAD BEEN DONE FOR GINX'S BABY?

The query would not have been very ridiculous. He was a unit of the British Empire: nothing could blot out that fact before heaven. Had any thing been left undone that ought to have been done, or done that had well been left undone, or were better to be undone now? Of a truth, that was worth a thought.

" What's all this? " said a big member of Parliament, — a minister renowned for economy in matters financial and intellectual. " What are you doing with this youngster? I never saw such an irregularity in a club in my life."

" If you saw it oftener, you would think more about it," said Sir Charles Sterling. " We found him on the steps. I think he was asking for you, Glibton."

This sally turned a laugh against the minister.

" Well," said another, " he has come to the wrong quarter if he wants money."

"I shouldn't wonder," said a third, "if he were one of the new messengers at the office of popular edifices. Glibton is reducing their staff."

"If that's the case, I think you have reached the *minimum* here, Glibton!" cried Sir Charles. "Can't the country afford a livery?"

"Bother you all!" replied the secretary, who was secretly pleased to be quizzed for his peculiarities: "tell us what this means. Whose 'lark' is it?"

"No lark at all," said Sterling. "Here is a problem for you and all of us to solve. This forlorn object is representative, and stands here to-night preaching us a serious sermon. He was deserted on the club steps, — left there, perhaps, as a piece of clever irony: he might be son to some of us. What's your name, my boy?"

Ginx's Baby managed to say "Dunno!"

"Ask him if he has any name," said an Irish ex-member with a grave face.

Ginx's Baby to this question responded distinctly "No."

"No name?" said the humorist: "then the author of his being must be Wilkie Collins."

Everybody laughed at this indifferent pleasantry but our hero. His bosom began to heave ominously.

"What's to be done with him?"

"Send him to the workhouse."

"Send him to the D——!" (there may be brutality among the gods and goddesses.)

"Give him to the porter."

"No, thank you, sir," said he promptly.

The gentlemen were turning away, when Sir Charles stopped them.

"Look here!" he said, taking the boy's arm, and bar-
ing it: "this boy can hardly be called a human being.
See what a thin arm he has! how flaccid and colorless
the flesh seems! what an old face!—and I can scarcely
feel any pulse. Good heavens! get him some wine. A
few hours will send him to the D—— sure enough. . . .
What are we to do for him, Glibton? I say again, he
is only part of a great problem. There must be hundreds of thousands growing up like this child; and
what a generation to contemplate in all its relations and
effects!"

The gentlemen were dashed by his earnestness.

"Oh! you're exaggerating," said Glibton: "there
can't be such widespread misery. Why, if there were,
the people would be wrecking our houses."

"Ah!" replied the other sadly, "will you wait to be
convinced by that sort of thing before you believe in
their misery? I assure you, what I say is true. I could
bring you a hundred clergymen to testify to it to-morrow
morning."

"God forbid!" said Glibton. "Good-night!"

The right honorable gentleman extinguished the
subject in his own little brain with his big hat: but
everywhere else the sparks are still aglow; and he, with
all like him, may wake up suddenly, as frightened
women in the night, to find themselves environed in the
red glare of a popular conflagration. Well for them
then if they are not in charge of the State machinery.
What an hour will that be for hurrying to and fro with
water-pipes and buckets, when proper forethought,
diligence, and sacrifice would have made the building
fireproof!

III. — A THOROUGH-PACED REFORMER, IF NOT A REVOLUTIONARY.

By the kindness and influence of Sir Charles Sterling, Ginx's Baby, that night, and long after, found shelter in the Radical Club. He gave rise to a discussion in the smoking-room next evening that ought to be chronicled. Several members of the committee supported his benefactor in urging that the child should be adopted by the club as a pledge of their resolve to make the questions of which he seemed to be the embodied emblem subjects of legislative action. Others said that those questions being, in their view, social, and not political, were not proper ones to give impulse to a party-movement; and that the entertainment in the club of this foundling would be a gross irregularity : they did not want samples of the material respecting which they were theorizing. To some of the latter Sir Charles had been insisting, that, whether they kept the child or not, they could not stifle the questions excited by his condition.

"You may delay, but you cannot dissipate them. We are filling up our sessions with party-struggles, theoretic discussions, squabbles about foreign politics, debates on political machinery, while year by year the condition of the people is becoming more invidious and full of peril. Social and political reform ought to be linked: the people on whom you confer new political rights cannot enjoy them without health and well-being."

"But all our legislation is directed to that!" exclaimed Mr. Joshua Hale. "Reform, free trade, free corn, — have these not enhanced the wealth of the people?"

"Partially; yet there are classes unregenerated by their reviving influences. Free trade cannot insure work, nor can free corn provide food, for every citizen."

"Nor any other legislation: let us be practical. I own there is much to be done. I have. often stated my 'platform.' We must clip the enormous expenditure on soldiers and ships; reduce our overweening army of diplomatic spies and busybodies; abstain from meddling in everybody's quarrels; redeem from taxation the workman's necessaries, — a free breakfast-table; peremptorily legislate against the custom of primogeniture; encourage the distribution and transfer of land; and, under the ægis of the ballot, protect from the tyranny of the landlord and employer their tenants and workmen."

" Very good, perhaps, all of them," replied Sir Charles; "but some not at the moment possible, and all together are not exhaustive. Why do you not go to the bottom of social needs? You say nothing about health legislation: are you indifferent to the sanitary condition of the people? You have not hinted at education, waste lands, emigration " —

" Oh! I am opposed to that altogether."

" I forgot: you are a manufacturer, yet the last man of whom I should believe that selfishness had warped the. judgment. You have done and endured more than any living statesman for the advantage of your fellow-citizens, so that I will not cast at you the aspersion of class-blindness. Still I can scarcely think you have looked at this matter in the pure light of patriotism, and not within the narrow scope of trade interests."

" Quite unjust. Our best economists reprehend the policy of depleting our labor-market. Emigration is a

timely remedy for adversity, and to be very sparingly
used. Labor is our richest vein " —

" We may have too much of it. Take it as a fact,
that you now have more than you can use, and the unem-
ployed part is starving : what will you do with them ? "

" That is a mere temporary and casual depression, to
which all classes are liable " —

" But," said Sir Charles, " which none can so ill bear.
Nay, what if it is permanent ? ' You look to increased
trade. Do you suppose we are to retain our manufac-
turing pre-eminence, when every country, new and old,
is competing with us ? Can our trade, I ask you honestly to consider, increase at the rate of our population ?
Besides, for Heaven's sake, look at the thing as a man !
Grant that we have a hundred thousand men out of
work, and hundreds of thousands more dependent on
them : do you think it no small thing that the vast
mass should be left for one, two, three years, seething in
sorrow and distress, while they are waiting for trade ?
By the time that comes, they may have gone beyond the
hope of rescue. Ah ! if an elastic trade comes back to-
morrow, you can never make those people what they
were : ought we not to have forecast that they should
not be what they are ? But I contend that depression
has become chronic, the poverty more wide-spread and
persistent : how, then, shall we, who represent these
classes among the rest, face the prospect ? "

Here interposed a gentleman high in office, a pure,
keen, rigid economist of the highest intellectual and political rank.

" My dear Sterling, pardon me if I say you are talking wildly. Perhaps you don't see that you are verging

on rank communism. The working of economic laws can be as infallibly projected as a solar eclipse. You can secure no class from periodic calamity, and so regulate laws of supply and demand by guiding-wheels of legislation and taxation as to save every man from penury. You wish us to send away our bone and sinew because we have no present employment for it; and next year, or the year after, under a recovered trade, you will be wringing your hands, and cursing the folly that prompted you to do it."

" I should be too glad of the opportunity," replied Sir Charles sturdily: "but, in truth, there is an incubus of excessive numbers, that no revival of trade will provide for, even if it is beyond our extremest hopes; and I, for one, will not be guilty of the inhumanity of keeping fellow-creatures in misery till we can find a use for them. You have forgotten that there are other economic laws besides those you glance at. Several millions of acres of unoccupied land, belonging, in a sense, to the people of this country, are to be kept untilled in defiance of the plainest policy that Nature and God have indicated to us; namely, that labor should come in contact with land. For want of this conjunction, our colonies are to be checked, while at home miserable millions are gaping for work and food."

" Oh! let them take themselves out. There are too many going already. They will follow natural laws; and where labor is required, thither the stream will flow."

" Mere surface-talk, my clever friend," replied the other. "The men who are trooping out at their own expense are our most sober, careful, and energetic workmen; else they could not go. They go because here so

many indifferent ones are weighing down their shoulders.
And where do most of them go to? Not to strengthen
and develop our colonies, but the United States, — a not
always friendly people, and, just now, your free-trader's
bugbear."

"Well, well," said the minister, "drop that question.
It's utterly impracticable at this time. We couldn't en-
tertain the demand for State-help for an instant. I tell
you again, you're a Fourierite. You virtually propose
to put your hand in the pocket of the upper classes to
pay all sorts of expenses for the lower."

"You may call me a communist, if you please," replied Sir Charles Sterling : "I do not shrink from shad-
ows. Perhaps I am in favor of something nearer to communism than our present form of society. One thing I
am clear about : no state of society is healthy wherein
every man does not own himself to be the guardian of
the interests of the community, as well as his own ;
does not see that he is bound, morally, and as a matter
of public policy, to add to his neighbor's well-being as
well as his own. Does not society, by its protection and
aggregation, make it possible for the rich to grow rich,
the genius and the ambitious man to pursue their aims,
the merchant to gather his vails, the noble to enjoy his
lands? For these privileges there is more or less to
pay ; and it may be that the proper proportion which the
capable classes should be called upon to contribute to the
common-weal has never been correctly adjusted. The
first-fruit of practical Christianity was community of
goods ; and, but for human selfishness, we might hope
for a Utopian era ; when, while it should be ruled, that
if a man would not work, neither should he eat, there

should also be brought home to every man the care of his poorer or weaker or less competent brother. I never expect to see that. I do hope to see the men of greatest ability pay more generously for the privileges they enjoy. The best policy for them too. The better the condition of the general community, the better for themselves. You cannot alarm me with epithets. But these views are, happily, not essential to the support of the emigration policy."

" Oh, dear! oh, dear! mad as a March hare!" cried the minister as he stumped from the room.

" Sterling is a good fellow," said he to a colleague with whom he walked down Pall Mall, " and a thorough-paced Liberal. Besides, he carries great weight in the House. But he is an enthusiast, and therefore not always quite practical."

By *practical*, the minister meant, not that which might well and to advantage be done if good and able men would resolve to do it, spite of all hinderances, but that which, upon a cunning review of party balances and a judicious probing of public opinion, seemed to be a policy fit for his party to pursue. The first, original and masterly statesmen are needed to initiate and perform : the other is simply the art of a genius who knows how most adroitly to manipulate people and circumstances.

IV.—Very Broad Views.

SIR CHARLES STERLING, Mr. Joshua Hale, and others continued the conversation interrupted by the minister's exit, — what was to be done with Ginx's Baby?

In the great dissected map of society, what niches were cut out for him, and all like him, to fill? Most of the politicians were for leaving that to himself to find out. The term, " law of supply and demand," was freely bandied between them, as it is in many journals nowadays, with little object save to shut up avenues of discussion by a high-sounding phrase.

Then, of these " statesmen," most clung, if not to self-interest, to personal crotchets. What is more darling to a man than the child of his intellect or fancy? How the poor poetaster hugs his tawdry verses, as if they were the imperial ornaments of genius! Just in the same way does the politician love the policies himself hath devised, pressing them forward at all hazards, while he is blind to the utility of others. This is the basis of that aspect of selfishness which often mars, in the approbation of a country, a really honest statesmanship, — an egotistic tenacity of one's own creature as the best, which yet is not the criminal selfishness of ambition. Still, that egotism is not seldom disastrous to the people's interests. While these statesmen nursed their own bantlings, and held them up to national notice, they were apt to avoid, or too lightly regard, the views of men as able as themselves. For instance, Joshua Hale — who is far above these remarks generally — had put forth a scheme for the solution of the St. Helena property question, — very likely a good one, albeit revolutionary; and nothing would convince him that any other could succeed. He wished every man in St. Helena (a turbulent adjunct of the British Empire) to be a landowner; and, I do think, neither desired nor hoped that any man in that island should be happy until he was one. Yet there

were other men ready to offer simpler remedies, and to
prove, that, if every man in St. Helena became a landowner, it would become a very hell upon earth, and more
unmanageable than it was before. If these gentlemen
do not sacrifice their pet fancies for the sake of a settlement, what will become of St. Helena?

Just now they were discussing Ginx's Baby. One
thought that repeal of the poor-laws and a new system
of relief would reach his case; another saw the root of
the baby's sorrow in trades' unions; a third pro-
pounded co-operative manufactures; a fourth suggested
that a vast source of income lay untouched in the seas
about the kingdom which swarmed with porpoises, and
showed how certain parts of these animals were available for food, others for leather, others for a delicious
oil that would be sweeter and more pleasant than butter;
a fifth desired a law to repress the tendency of Scotch
peers to evict tenants, and convert arable lands into
sheep-walks and deer-forests; a sixth maintained that
there were waste lands in the kingdom, of capacity to
support hungry millions. In fact, earth, heaven, and
seas were to be regenerated by act of Parliament for
the benefit of Ginx's Baby and the people of England.
Sir Charles listened impatiently, and at last burst forth
again.

He said, "When you consider it, what we are all
trying to do nowadays is — vulgarly — to improve the
breed; but we go to work in a roundabout way. At
the outset, we are met by the depreciated state of part
of the existing generation; and one problem is to prevent these depreciated people from increasing, or to get
them to increase healthily. No one seems to have gone

directly to such a problem as that. The difficulties to be faced are tremendous. Your dirtiest British youngster is hedged round with principles of an inviolable liberty and rights of *habeas corpus.* You let his father and mother, or any one who will save you the trouble of looking after him, mould him in his years of tenderness as they please. If they happen to leave him a walking invalid, you take him into the poorhouse; if they bring him up a thief, you whip him, and keep him at high cost at Millbank or Dartmoor; if his passions, never controlled, break out into murder and rape, you may hang him, unless his crime has been so atrocious as to attract the benevolent interest of the Home Secretary; if he commit suicide, you hold a coroner's inquest, which also costs money; and, however he dies, you give him a deal coffin, and bury him. Yet I may prove to you that this being, whom you treat like a dog at a fair, never had a day's, no, nor an hour's, contact with goodness, purity, truth, or even human kindness; never had an opportunity of learning any thing better. What right have you, then, to hunt him like a wild beast, and kick him and whip him, and fetter him, and hang him by expensive complicated machinery, when you have done nothing to teach him any of the duties of a citizen?

" Stop, stop, Sir Charles! you are too virulent. There are endless means of improving your lad, — charities without number " —

" Yes, that will never reach him."

" Never mind: they may, you know. Industrial schools, reformatories, asylums, hospitals, Peabody-buildings, poor-laws. Everybody is working to improve the condition of the poor man. Sanitary administration goes to his house, and makes it habitable."

" Very ! " interjected Sir Charles Sterling dryly.

" Factory-laws protect and educate factory-children " —

" They don't educate in one case out of ten. They don't feed them, clothe them, give them amusement and cultivation, do they ? "

" Certainly not ! That would be ridiculous ! "

" Why, the question is, whether that would be ridiculous," replied Sir Charles. " I do not say it can be done ; but, in order to transform the next generation, what we should aim at is to provide substitutes for bad homes, evil training, unhealthy air, food and dulness, and terrible ignorance, in happier scenes, better teaching, proper conditions of physical life, sane amusements, and a higher cultivation. I dare say you would think me a lunatic if I proposed that government should establish music-halls and gymnasia all over the country ; but you, Mr. Fissure, voted for the baths and wash-houses."

" Who's to pay for all this ? " asked Mr. Fissure pertinently.

" The State, which means society ; the whole of which is directly interested. I tell you, a million of children are crying to us to set them free from the despotism of a crime and ignorance protected by law."

" That is striking ; but you are treading on delicate ground. The liberty of the subject " —

" Exactly what I expected you to say. These words can be used in defence of almost any injustice and tyranny. Such terms as ' political economy,' ' communism,' ' socialism,' are bandied about in the same way. Yet propositions coming fairly within these terms are often mentioned with approval by the very persons who cast them at you. In a report of a recent royal commission, I find that one of the commissioners is quite as revolutionary as I am. He says it is right by law to secure that no child shall be cruelly treated or mentally neglected, over-worked or under-educated. Some people would call that communism, I fancy; but I think him to be correct as a political economist in that broad proposition. Why? Because a child's relation to the State is wider, more permanent, and more important, than his relation to his parents. If he is in danger of being depreciated and damned for good citizenship, the State must rescue him."

"A paternal and maternal government together!" cries Lord Namby, — "a government of nurses. You know I should like to stop the production of children among the lower orders. Your propositions are far in advance of my radicalism. The State must sometimes interfere between parent and child; for instance, in education, or protection from cruelty. But, if I understand you, you actually contemplate a general refining and elevation of the working-class by legislative means."

"Assuredly! I should aim to cultivate their morals, refine their tastes, manners, habits. I wish to lift from them that ever-depressing sense of hopelessness which keeps them in the dust."

"So do most men; but you must do that by personal and private influences, not by State enactments. How would you do it?"

"How? I think I could draw up a programme. For instance: Expatriate a million to reduce the competition that keeps poor devils on half-rations, or sends them to the poor-house; take all the sick, maimed, old, and incapable poor, into workhouses managed by humane men, and not by ghouls; forbid such people to marry and propagate weakness; legislate for compulsory improvements of workmen's dwellings, — and, if needful, lend the money to execute it; extend and enforce the health laws; open free libraries and places of rational amusement with an imperial bounty through the country; instead of spending thousands on *dilettanti* sycophants at one end of the metropolis, distribute your art and amusement to the kingdom at large; the rich have their museums, libraries, and clubs; provide them for the poor; establish temporary homes for lying-in women; multiply your baths and washhouses till there is no excuse for a dirty person; educate; provide day-schools for every proper child, and industrial or reformatory schools for every improper one; open advanced high schools for the best pupils, and found scholarships to the universities; erect other schools for technical training; offer to teach trades and agriculture to all comers for nothing, — you would soon neutralize your bugbear of trade's-unionism; teach morals, teach science, teach art, teach them to amuse themselves like men, and not like brutes. In a land so wealthy, the programme is not impracticable, though severe. As the end to be attained is the welfare of future generations, no good reason could be urged why they should not contribute towards the cost of it, — a better debt to leave to posterity than the incubus of an irrational war."

Will any sane political practitioner wonder to be told, that, at the end of this harangue, the smoking-room party broke up, and that some, as they laughed good-humoredly over Sterling's *egregia*, recalled the number of glasses of inspirited seltzer swallowed by the orator ? He was so far in advance of the most radical reformer, that there was no hope of overtaking him for an era or two : so they determined to fancy they had left him behind.

———◆———

V.—PARTY TACTICS, AND POLITICAL OBSTRUCTIONS TO SOCIAL REFORM.

IN the club, our hero revelled a while under the protection of Sir Charles Sterling, and the petting of peers, members of Parliament, and loungers who swarm therein. Certain gentlemen of Stock-Exchange mannerism and dressiness gave the *protégé* the go-by, and even sneered at those who noticed him with kindness. But then these are of the men with whom every question is checked by money, and is balanced on the pivot of profit and loss. I dare say some of them thought the worse of Judas only because he had made so small a gain out of his celebrated transaction. To foster Ginx's Baby in the club as a recognition of the important questions surrounding him, though these questions involved hundreds of thousands of other cases, was to them ridiculous. Of far greater consequence was it, in their eyes, to settle a dispute between two extravagant fools at Constantinople and Cairo, and quicken the sluggishness of Turkish consols or Egyptian 9 per cents. I do not cast stones at them : every man must look at a thing with his own eyes.

But it was curious to note how the baby's fortunes

shifted in the club. There were times when he was a
pet chucked under chin by the elder stagers, favored
with a smile from a cabinet minister, and now and then
blessed with a nod from Mr. Joshua Hale.   Then,
again, every one seemed to forget him; and he was for
months left unnoticed to the chance-kindness of the
menials, until, some case similar to his own happening to
evoke discussion in the press, there would be a general
inquiry for him.   The porter, Mr. Smirke, had succeeded, by means of a detective, in discovering the boy's
name; but his parents were then half-way to Canada.

The members of the Fogy Club opposite, hearing
that so interesting a foundling was being cherished by
their opponents, politely asked leave to examine him;
and he occasionally visited them.   They treated him
kindly, and discussed his condition with earnestness.
The leaders of the party debated whether he might not,
with advantage, be taken out of their opponents' hands.
Some thought that a judicious use of him might win
popularity; but others objected that it would be perilous
for them to mix themselves up with so doleful an interest.   In the result, the Fogies tipped young Ginx, but
did not commit themselves for or against him.   Thus a
long time elapsed; and our hero had grown old enough
to be a page.   He had received food, clothing, and
good will; but no one had thought of giving him an
education.   Sometimes he became obstreperous.   He
played tricks with the club cutlery, and diverted its
silver to improper uses; he laid traps for upsetting
aged and infirm legislators; he tried the coolness of the
youngest and best-natured members of Parliament by
popping up in strange places, and exhibiting unseemly

attitudes. At length, by unanimous consent, he was decreed to be a nuisance, and a few days would have revoked his license at the club.

No sooner did the Fogies get wind of this than they manœuvred to get Ginx's Baby under their own management. They instructed their "organs," as they called them, to pipe to popular feeling on the disgraceful apathy of the Radicals in regard to the foundling. They had him waylaid and treated to confectionery by their emissaries; and once or twice succeeded in abducting him, and sending him down to the country with their party's candidates, for exhibition at elections.

The Radicals resented this conduct extremely. Ginx's Baby was brought back to the club, and restored to favor. The government papers were instructed to detail how much he was petted and talked about by the party; to declare how needless was the popular excitement on his behalf; and to prove that he must, without any special legislation, be benefited by the extraordinary organic changes then being made in the constitution of the country.

Sir Charles Sterling resumed his interest in the boy. He had been gallantly aiding his party in other questions. There was the Timbuctoo question. A miserable desert chief had shut up a wandering Englishman not possessed of wit enough to keep his head out of danger. There was a general impression that English honor was at stake; and the previous Fogy government had ordered an expedition to cross the desert, and punish the sheik. You would never believe what it cost if you had not seen the bill. Ten millions sterling was as good as buried in the desert, when one-tenth of it would have saved a hundred thousand people from starvaticn at home, and one hundredth part of it would have taken the fetters off the hapless prisoner's feet.

There was the St. Helena question always brooding over Parliament. St. Helena was a constituent part of the British Empire. Every patriot agreed that the empire without it would be incomplete; and was so far right, that its subtraction would have left the empire by so much less. Most of its inhabitants were aboriginal, — a mercurial race, full of fire, quick-witted, and gifted with the exuberant eloquence of savages, but deficient in dignity and self-control. Before any one else had been given them by Providence to fight, they slaughtered and ravaged one another. Our intrusive British ancestors stepped upon the island, and, being strong men, mowed down the islanders like wheat, and appropriated the lands their swords had cleared. Still the aborigines held out in corners, and defied the conquerors. The latter ground them down, confiscated the property of their half-dozen chiefs, and distributed it among themselves. By way of showing their imperial imperiousness, they built over some ruins left by their devastations a great church, in which they ordered all the islanders to worship. This was at first abomination to the islanders, who fought like devils whenever they could, and ended by accepting the religion of their foes. But the conquerors, afterwards choosing to change their own faith, resolved that the islanders should do so too. Forthwith they confiscated the big church and burying-ground, and, distributing part of the land and spoils among their most prominent scamps, erected a new edifice of quite a different character, in which the

natives swore they could neither see nor hear, and their
own clerics warned them they would certainly be
damned.   To make the complications more intricate,
these clerics owed allegiance to an ancient woman in a
distant country, who had all the meddlesomeness and
petty jealousy of her sex, and was, besides, much at-
tached to some clever wooers of hers, — wily sinners who
covered their aims under the semblance of ultra-extreme
passion for her.   The prominent scamps died, to be succeeded by their children, or other of the hated conquerors, from generation to generation.   The islanders
went on increasing and protesting.   They starved upon
the lands, and shot the landlords when a few gave them
the chance ; for most lived away in their own country,
and left the property to be administered by agents.   The
home government had again and again been obliged to
assist these people with soldiers, to provide an armed
police, to shoot down mobs, to catch a ringleader here
or there and send him to Fernando Po, or to deprive
whole villages of ordinary civil rights.   Then the yam-
crop failed, and nearly half the people left the island
and crossed the seas, where they continued to hate and
to plot against those whose misfortune it had been to
get a legacy of the island from their fathers.   It would
be wearisome to recount the absurdities on both sides,
the stupidity or criminal absence of tact from time to
time shown by the home government, the resolve never
to be quiet exhibited by the natives, under the prompt-
ing of their clerics.   Upon

" That common stage of novelty "

there were ever springing up fresh difficulties.   Secret

clubs were formed for murder and reprisal. A body
called the "Yellows" had bound themselves by private
oaths to keep up the memory of the religious victories of
their predecessors, and to worry the clerical party in
every possible way. Their pleasure was to go about in-
sanely blowing rams'-horns, carrying flags, and bearing
oranges in their hands. The islanders hated oranges,
and at every opportunity cracked the skulls of the
orange-bearers with brutal weapons peculiar to the
island. These, in return, cracked native skulls. The
whole island was in a state of perpetual commotion.
Still its general condition improved, its farms grew
prosperous; and a joint-stock company had built a mill
for converting cocoanut-fibre into horse-cloths, which
yielded large profits. The memory of past events might
well have been buried : but the clerics, in the interest of
the old woman, fanned the embers ; and the infamous
bidding for popularity of parties at home served to keep
alive passions that would naturally have died out. Besides, latterly, folly had been too organized on both
sides to suffer oblivion. Everybody was tired of the
squabbles of St. Helena. At length there was a general
movement in the interests of peace; and, to pacify the
islanders, Parliament was asked to pull down the wings
of the old church-edifice, remove some of the graves,
and cut off a large piece of the graveyard. Some were
in favor, also, of dividing all the farms in the country
among the aborigines; but the difficulty was, to know
how, at the same time, to satisfy the present occupiers.
These schemes were topics of high debate; upon them
the fortunes of government rose and fell ; and, while
they were agitated, Ginx's Baby could have no chance
of a parliamentary hearing.

Many other matters of singular indifference had eaten up the legislative time : but at last the increasing number of wretched infants throughout the country began to alarm the people ; and Sir Charles Sterling thought the time had come to move on behalf of Ginx's Baby and his fellows.

———◆———

VI.—Amateur Debating in a High Legislative Body.

While Sir Charles was trying to get the government to " give him a night " to debate the Ginx's Baby case, and while associations were being formed in the metropolis for disposing of him by expatriation or otherwise, a busy peer, without notice to anybody, suddenly brought the subject before the House of Lords. As he had never seen the baby, and knew nothing, or very little, about him, I need scarcely report the elaborate speech in which he asked for aristocratic sympathy on his behalf. He proposed to send him to the antipodes at the expense of the nation.

The Minister for the Accidental Accompaniments of the Empire was a clever man, — keen, genial, subtle, two-edged ; a gentlemanly and not thorough disciple of Machiavel ; able to lead parliamentary forlorn hopes, and plant flags on breaches, or to cover retreats with brilliant skirmishing ; deft, but never deep ; much moved, too, by the opinions of his permanent staff. These, on the night in question, had plied him well with hackneyed objections ; but to see him get up and relieve himself of them — the air of originality, the really original air he threw around them, the absurd light which he turned full on the weaknesses of his noble friend's propositions — was as beautiful to an indifferent critic as it was saddening to the man who had at heart the sorrows of his kind. If that minister lived long, he would be forced to adopt and advocate in as pretty a manner the policy he was dissecting.

Lord Munnibagge, a great authority in economic matters, said that a weaker case had never been presented to Parliament. To send away Ginx's Baby to a colony, at imperial expense, was at once to rob the pockets of the rich, and to decrease our labor-power. There was no necessity for it. Ginx's Baby could not starve in a country like this. He (Lord Munnibagge) had never heard of a case of a baby starving. There was no such widespread distress as was represented by the noble lord. There were occasional periods of stagnation in trade; and no doubt, in these periods, the poorer classes would suffer: but trade was elastic; and, even if it were granted that the present was a period when employment had failed, the time was not far off when trade would recuperate. (Cheers.) Ginx's Baby, and all other babies, would not then wish to go away. People were always making exaggerated statements about the condition of the poor. He (Lord Munnibagge) did not credit them. He believed the country, though temporarily depressed by financial collapses, to be in a most healthy state. (Hear, hear.) It was absurd to say otherwise, when it was shown by the board-of-trade returns that we were growing richer every day. (Cheers.) Of course, Ginx's Baby must be growing richer with the rest. Was not that a complete answer to the noble lord's plaintive outcries? (Cheers and laughter.) That the population of a country was

a great fraction of its wealth was an elementary principle of political economy. He thought, from the high
rates of wages, that there were not too many, but too
few, laborers in the country. He should oppose the
motion. (Cheers.)

Two or three noble lords repeated similar platitudes,
guarding themselves as carefully from any reference to
facts, or to the question whether high rates of wages
might not be the concomitants simply of high prices of
necessaries, or to the yet wider question whether colo-
nial development might not have something to do with
progress at home. The noble lord who had rushed un-
prepared into the arena was unequal to the forces mar-
shalled against him, and withdrew his motion.

Thus the great debate collapsed. The lords were relieved that an awkward question had so easily been
shifted. The newspapers on the ministerial side declared
that this debate had proved the futility of the Ginx's
Baby expatriation question.

" So able an authority as Lord Munnibagge had established that there was no necessity for the interference of
government in the case of Ginx's Baby or any other
babies or persons. The lucid and decisive statement
of the Secretary for the Accidental Accompaniments of
the Empire had shown how impossible it was for the imperial government to take part in a great scheme of expatriation; how impolitic to endeavor to affect the
ordinary laws of free movement to the colonies."

Surely, after this, the expatriation people hid their
lights under a bushel !

The government refused to find a night for Sir Charles
Sterling; and, after the Lords' debate, he did not see his

way to force a motion in the Lower House. Meanwhile
Ginx's Baby once more decided a turn in his own fate.
Tired of the slow life of the club, and shivering amid the
chill indifference of his patrons, he borrowed, without
leave, some clothes from an inmate's room, with a few
silver forks and spoons, and decamped. Whether the
baronet and the club were bashful of public ridicule, or
glad to be rid of the charge, I know not; but no attempt
was made to recover him.

PART V.

WHAT GINX'S BABY DID WITH HIMSELF.

> " A full-formed horse will, in any market, bring from twenty to
> as high as two hundred Friedrichs d'or: such is his worth to the
> world. A full-formed man is not only worth nothing to the world,
> but the world could afford him a round sum would he simply engage
> to go and hang himself." — SARTOR RESARTUS.

THE LAST CHAPTER.

OUR hero was nearly fifteen years old when he left
the club to plunge into the world. He was not
long in converting his spoils into money, and a very
short time in spending it. Then he had to pit his wits
against starvation; and some of his throws were desper-
ate. Wherever he went, the world seemed terribly full.
If he answered an advertisement for an errand-boy, there
were a score kicking their heels at the rendezvous
before him. Did he try to learn a useful trade, thousands of adepts were not only ready to underbid him,
but to knock him on the head for an interloper. Even
the thieves, to whom he gravitated, were jealous of his
accession, because there were too many competitors
already in their department. Through his career of
penury, of honest and dishonest callings, of 'scapes and

captures, imprisonments and other punishments, a year's reading of metropolitan police-reports would furnish the exact counterpart.

———————

I don't know how many years after his flight from Pall Mall, one dim midnight, I, returning from Richmond, lounged over Vauxhall Bridge, listening to the low lapping of the current beneath the arches; looking above to the stars, and along the dark polished surface that reflected a thousand lights in its undulations; feeling the awfulness of the dense, suppressed life that was wrapped within the gloom and calm of the hour. I suddenly saw a shadow, a human shadow, that, at the sound of my footstep, quickly crossed my dreamy vision,— quickly, noiselessly came and went before my eyes, until it stood up high and outlined against the strangely-mingled haze. It looked like the ghost of a slight-formed man, hatless and coatless; and for a moment I saw at its upper extremity the dull flash as of a human face in the gloom, before the shadow leaped out far into the night. Splash! When my startled eyes looked down upon the glancing, waving ebony, I thought I could trace a white coruscation of foam spreading out into the darkness, instantly to dissipate and be lost forever.

I did not then know what form it was that swilled down below the glistening current. Had I known that it was Ginx's Baby, I should perhaps have thought, "Society, which, in the sacred names of Law and Charity, forbade the father to throw his child over Vauxhall Bridge at a time when he was alike unconscious of life and death, has at last itself driven him over the parapet into the greedy waters" ——

Philosophers, philanthropists, politicians, Papists and Protestants, poor-law ministers and parish-officers, while you have been theorizing and discussing, debating, wrangling, legislating, and administering, — Good God! gentlemen, between you all, where has Ginx's Baby gone to?